THE GIRL IN THE VIDEO

MICHAEL DAVID WILSON

PMMP

Perpetual Motion Machine Publishing
Cibolo, Texas

The Girl in the Video

ISBN: 978-1-943720-43-9

www.PerpetualPublishing.com

Cover Art by Pye Parr
www.pyeparr.com

ADVANCE PRAISE FOR THE GIRL IN THE VIDEO

"Propulsive, modern, funny, frightening. *The Girl in the Video* will make you think twice about opening any anonymous videos sent your way. Then it'll make you think twice again. Michael David Wilson has long added to the genre with his incredible podcast/press *This is Horror*, but here he offers a book, and now it's time for someone else to interview him."

—Josh Malerman,
New York Times bestselling author of *Bird Box*,
Unbury Carol, and *A House at the Bottom of a Lake*

"*The Girl in the Video* took me somewhere I didn't want to go via a route I didn't want to take. It's an unsettling story of love, lust, and cultural disorientation that'll flirt with you and then, when you're at your most vulnerable, take full advantage of your good intentions."

—David Moody,
author of *Autumn* and *Hater*

"Compelling, tense, and disturbing, Michael David Wilson has created a frightening story here that's only too possible in our over-connected world."

—Alan Baxter,
the award-winning author of *Served Cold* and the
Alex Caine series

For all the teachers in the world who inspire and encourage creativity, including George Ttoouli who once described my fiction as 'horrific, depraved, hilarious, and offensive'. I hope I've done you proud.

I'M TIRED OF TRYING to pinpoint where, how, or why this mess started. But for the sake of brevity, let's focus on an early October morning in 2015 and a peculiar message. It was that rare time of year when the temperature inside the house was near perfect, neither hot enough for air conditioning nor cold enough for the heater. I was downstairs, in the room that served as both a kitchen and lounge, cooking breakfast. Rachel sat at the table, engrossed in her iPad. The back door was cracked open, the autumn chill dancing with the scent of fried bacon and strong coffee. In the distance, the hum of schoolchildren doing their morning exercises on the nearby playground. And by 'nearby' I mean practically affixed to the bottom of the patio. And by 'patio' I mean a strip of concrete you'd be lucky to fit a barbecue on. There was a fence and everything. All above board. Nothing dodgy. I wasn't renting a house that included a school, but anyway, I digress . . .

I brought the breakfast to the table—each plate loaded with poached eggs, spinach, two rashers of bacon, mushrooms, and a fried tomato. Rachel was still in 'Christ, it's early, drink all the coffee' mode, shortly she'd transition to 'oh shit, look at the time, better get ready for work' mode. She wore pink and white pyjamas punctuated with grey cartoon cats, her dark chocolate hair scraped back into a tight bun. I cracked a little sea salt onto my eggs, Rachel shook a generous helping of salt and pepper onto absolutely everything. Ulver streamed through the Bluetooth speakers, an instrumental album I cared for and Rachel did not.

By-and-large, it was a pleasant enough morning.

I poured us both a cup of coffee, from an olive wood French press, and Rachel said: "Period came this morning."

Now granted, that wasn't a conventional response, a simple 'cheers for the coffee' would have done nicely, but neither of us cared much for convention. And besides, we were comfortable—together for over ten years, married for five.

"Well, it's okay, we're still young. There's time," I said.

"Be a darling and get some cream from the fridge, would you?"

I did as she asked, reattaching the crayoned drawing that frayed at the edges, a present from a former student.

"Cheers." Rachel added cream to her coffee, stirred. "Best not to get our hopes up, though. Even if I do test positive, could be a phantom pregnancy."

"Like a ghost baby?"

"No, dumbass." Followed by a grin that extended to her eyes. "A phantom pregnancy's when you display all the signs of pregnancy but aren't actually pregnant."

"Guess that's why they wait longer for the ultrasound back in England. What is it? Eight weeks? Earlier? Later than here, at any rate. Akane got hers at five weeks, maybe less."

"A phantom pregnancy can last way longer than

eight weeks. There've been cases where women have been convinced they're pregnant for the full nine months."

"Sounds far-fetched—you'd think the absence of a bump would be the key piece to that particular puzzle."

"There's actually abdominal swelling, you know."

"But surely not nine-month 'someone call me a doctor because mummy's-about-to-burst' swelling."

She rolled her eyes. "There's *a lot* about it online—fascinating reading."

"Perhaps you read too much."

"All right, *Dr. Sapirstein*." We'd watched *Rosemary's Baby* a few nights previous.

"Come on, *Rosemary*. Drink up your coffee, and don't you mind the chalky under-taste, bit of tannis root never hurt anyone."

After breakfast and washing-up, Rachel showered, singing Lady Gaga songs so loud the whole neighbourhood could hear. I took my phone from my pocket and went through my periodic ritual of cycling through social media apps. Twitter to WhatsApp to Twitter again—wouldn't want to miss anything in those valuable seconds—to Hello Talk to Instagram, back to Twitter, and just as I thought I couldn't hate myself or other people more I'd check Facebook. Rachel said I had a strange relationship with social media. That I should delete it if it brought me so much anxiety and despair. But it's swings and roundabouts. How else was I supposed to know that Louis from middle school had mown his lawn, or that Carys, who I hadn't seen in fifteen years, was holidaying in Malaga. And without Facebook I certainly wouldn't have seen a picture of Thornby's breakfast—Cheerios every day for the past two weeks. That's not even exaggeration, the guy posted a bowl of Cheerios daily, even giving them a rating out of ten, no half marks, integers only.

I didn't see it at first, but on a second round of social media cycling, I noticed a new Instagram direct message from some random with a Hello Kitty display pic.

The message was short: *a late birthday present.*

Below lay a shortened Bitly web address concealing the original URL.

Now usually I wouldn't click obscured links from randoms, but whatever the reason—slip of the finger, lapse of judgement, overwhelmed from Thornby's constant barrage of fucking Cheerios—I put on my headphones and did just that. Took a while to buffer, but eventually a video just over five minutes long appeared.

The camera focused on a girl sitting on a leather office chair. Only her lower body visible to the camera. Smooth toned legs in fishnets, crossed and uncrossed, crossed and uncrossed, always right leg over left, in sync with the music. I recognised the tune straight away but couldn't quite place it. Something from my uni days. The track began dramatically— electronic and pulsating—an energetic piece that commanded attention.

The legs commanded attention, too—swinging frenetically.

THE GIRL IN THE VIDEO

The music slowed into a jazzy number—something sexier, the legs mirroring the music.

Low key vocals crept in.

I strained to hear the lyrics, unable to decipher anything until:

"What's the meaning of this voyage?"

And that's when it hit me. Ulver! We'd listened to them at breakfast, minutes ago. Though this was from a different album. An older album.

I racked my brain because it seemed important.

An opening track, not from *Blood Inside*. Earlier than that, so . . .

Perdition City! That was it.

Momentary elation was quick to subside—I didn't feel any better for knowing.

At the three-minute mark, the girl hummed along to the tune. Her voice vanilla icing, so sweet and so soft.

Satin silky legs continued to cross and uncross.

The camera zoomed out and her full profile revealed itself for the first time. The small swell of her breasts underneath a black blouse. The short black skirt and studded belt. The cardboard Hello Kitty mask that concealed the upper half of her face. Guessed she was in her late teens or early twenties. But with the mask and the grainy camera, the relative dark and the large shadows, it was difficult to be sure.

On her feet, the girl swayed her hips to the beat. Movements slow and loose.

Delicate.

Alluring.

Sensual.

Five minutes in, the video cut from full colour to

monochrome, save for a pair of pink plump lips. The focal point.

The camera zoomed out. The girl seated once more. She dipped a thin lip brush into a tube of lip lacquer and painted her pink lips sanguine.

So fresh and so wet I could almost smell the varnish.

She applied the lipstick again-and-again, like the crossing and uncrossing of her legs, always in time with the music.

When the music stopped, I realised I'd fallen into a trance, mesmerised by her calm and deliberate movements.

Relaxing.

Meditative.

Freeing.

Ten seconds of the video remained.

A final close-up of the girl's lips and in a voice so soft it was barely audible she whispered, "Happy belated birthday."

I don't know how long I stood there—caught in a daze, phone in my hand, headphones still on. I full-on jolted when Rachel re-entered the room, a light grey towel wrapped around her body. She said, "Remember to take the plastic—*bloody hell!*"

I followed Rachel's gaze to my . . . *oh Jesus Christ*, I had a massive stork on.

"Now I know I look good, 'n'all," Rachel said, "the whole wet hair, bags under the eyes, and old towel thing is pretty hot right now—and I'm flattered you're *so* happy to see me—but I don't think there's time." She winked. "Unlike you with your late Monday timetable, I'm on an early—first lesson's at twelve. I've got to leave in twenty minutes."

THE GIRL IN THE VIDEO

"Umm . . . " I searched for something smart to say, something that was definitely not, *just watched a bizarre and* evidently *arousing video* . . . "Just thought since we both want to be parents so bad we should seize every opportunity."

I cringed at my words—bloody hell, should have stuck with the whole arousing video thing. At least Rachel was grinning. "You *do* remember I'm on my period, right?"

"Yeah, but, I mean, might be a phantom period . . . "

She smiled—probably out of pity—then made her way upstairs.

Seconds later she called, "But seriously, Freddie, don't forget to take the plastic out, yeah?"

I ran to the bathroom and shot my load.

With each viewing of the video, I found myself in a light trance as I enjoyed how well the visuals complemented the music. Sure, it was an amateur production, no doubt put together using cheap editing software. And yet there seemed to be something deeper to it, something *more*. It took a great deal of mental strength not to jack off there and then. Acting on my impulses would be a step too far. I didn't want to debase the art, didn't want to spoil the 'belated birthday present'.

Chances were the video was just spam—this kind of shit happens all the time—and yet maybe, just maybe, it really was a late birthday present. Very late given my birthday had been back in August, but I was pretty bad at replying to emails and everything seemed to take way longer these days, not least if it had been sent from abroad.

Then again this is the fucking internet, there shouldn't be a delay from abroad.

Well, whatever. Whether it was or wasn't a birthday present, whether it was or wasn't sent from overseas—I wasn't gonna degrade it and myself.

But I *was* saving the file.

I opened my MacBook and used some browser extension to extract the video. Saved it in my 'important administrative work' folder with all the rest of my 'important' videos.

In the days that followed I played the video numerous times, but as days became weeks and weeks months, I mostly forgot about it, moving onto other things to obsess over.

SATURDAY JANUARY 23, 2016

My favourite burger bar in Japan is this neat little joint in Ryogoku, called Shake Tree. It's a bit off the beaten track, but the quality and variety make it well worth a visit. They even do a lettuce wrap or extra burger patties if you don't want bread, and if you're looking for an eating challenge, they've got you covered. Just keep adding those patties, loading up on bacon, heaping up cheese, avocadoes, eggs, you name it—because if you've got the money, they've got the food.

So, that's where we went—Rachel and I—on a rare Saturday off work, making the most of the extra time together. I tucked into a juicy burger with melted cheese, a thick slice of ripe tomato, and a slither of gherkin for added zest. The burger oozed grease which I dipped the fries in—trust me, it tastes great— even treated myself to a glass of Maker's Mark. Rachel had one of those double burgers with the extra bacon and creamy avocado add-on. A banana milkshake ice cream-like consistency really sealed the deal.

"You sure this is the right time?" I asked. "It's just, I imagined it a little differently. That we'd have everything in order. Or not *everything*, but at least a mortgage and a fat wad of cash in the bank. Savings, I mean."

"A mortgage means you owe some big corporation a shit-load of money for decades. A mortgage is a whole heap of debt. Look at what happened to Hillary—borrowed eight times her salary just before the financial crisis, and now she can't afford to sell the bloody thing. Trust me, no mortgage is a good thing."

"I guess . . . but we should have a forever home . . . " I paused. "Wrong expression. Think forever home's for pets, but you know what I mean . . . More stability. All we have now is a three-year visa. What if we have to uproot? What if we need to go back to England? Or decide to move someplace else? I've always wondered about Denmark."

"Then we'll do it. We'll look at our options and make the right decision for us at the time. But right now, we're here and we're happy. Aren't we?"

I nodded and it was honest. We were happy.

Rachel reached across the table and squeezed my hand. "What's gotten into you? You're usually the one reassuring me, not the other way around."

"I'm a little scared about being a dad. Felt the same before we got married. I get this tiny pang of sickness in the pit of my stomach just thinking about it, in case I mess up." I sighed, didn't want to bring the mood down but owed it to Rachel to be real. "What it comes down to is I'm afraid of commitment. Making the wrong decisions. Decisions that can't be undone . . . And I'm pretty sure we can't put the child back in once it comes out."

Rachel laughed. "Put it back in? You're terrible."

"It's true! I mean, physically, we could try but I expect it'll kick up a fuss and then there's the nurses, what will they say?" I dabbed my upper lip with a serviette, wiping away burger residue. "Seriously, though, part of me is so up for being a dad—the first time we see our kid, holding its little hand, pressing our kid close to my chest, giving it all the love I craved as a child but never quite got, taking all my life lessons and giving it my best shot." I knocked back a mouthful of bourbon. "But the other part . . . well, the other part thinks I'm gonna fuck it up royally, because honestly that's what I do. I fuck things up. Don't want my kid to become another fuck-up in a long list of fuck-ups. This—having a kid—is for real, you know. It's not like some dumb night out, a poor turn of phrase, or a questionable business decision. We're talking about human life—you don't get to erase the slate and start again, you make a mistake and that's permanent damage."

Rachel took a moment. "You're too hard on yourself. And you're allowed to make mistakes, we all are, it's part of being human." The waitress approached, probably to ask 'is everything's all right with your food', but promptly turned away when she realised the seriousness of the conversation. "I'm scared, too. And for what it's worth I think you'll be a great father. A *dad*. You'll fuck up, sure, and I'll fuck up, too. And we'll fuck up together, and sometimes we'll fuck up separately by contradicting one another's fuck-ups, but on the whole, we'll do well. We'll get through the tough times. We always do. I just wish *you* believed in *you* as much as I do."

"That's sweet, Rach. Really. I appreciate it."

"I'm serious. And the money, the mortgage, there being a perfect time . . . it's all bollocks. You're the one who told me that, remember? There are times that are better than others, sure, but there isn't a *perfect* time. Sometimes you've got to take the leap. And right now, we're in a decent position. We've got money in the bank—granted, not a lot—and we're saving a little every month, we're never hungry, we always pay our bills on time, and we're living in a country we love, doing work we love. Not perfect, but pretty damn good. Better than most."

"I guess."

"You *know*. Plus, we've been over this before, worked out the timing and everything. As long as I'm pregnant in the next few months, I'll go on maternity leave and return to work before my contract's up for renewal. The school might not pay maternity but they can't refuse my leave. It's set-in-stone. It's the law."

"Such bullshit we even have to think about it. I mean, it's good we've considered all the possibilities, sensible even, but it's still bullshit."

"A lot of things in this world are." Rachel picked up her iPhone. "Now pose with what's left of the burger, I wanna take a snap."

"Want me to put my arm around it like we're best mates?"

"You dumbass—just hold it up or something."

"Give it a little kiss, maybe?"

She sighed and gave me a look like perhaps she had reservations about the whole baby idea, after all.

After taking a handful of photographs and uploading the best to Instagram, we finished our meals and ordered coffee. Rachel popped to the bathroom and I perused Twitter, minding my own business and keeping my head down. I snapped to attention when some customer's ringtone sounded off: 'Lost In Moments' by Ulver. The damn thing made me jolt up so hard I almost fell out of my chair and smashed my bloody phone at the same time. I steadied myself, spun around to look for the offending customer but came up short. I scanned the rest of the restaurant: the patrons, the waiters, the bar staff, but couldn't identify where or who the song came from. I even looked down at my own phone to check I hadn't been a right dickhead and accidentally played the track myself— navigating to Spotify then Apple Music just to be sure.

The song soon faded and Rachel returned.

"Did you hear it?"

"Huh?"

"Did you hear it? The music."

Rachel strained to listen. "Nickelback, isn't it?"

"No. Well, yeah, but I'm not talking about *that* music. You hear the *ringtone*? Someone has Ulver as their ringtone."

"Oh. I don't know anything about that."

"Shit. I have to know whose ringtone that was."

"*Have to*, eh? Better stand up and make an announcement." Rachel grinned. Her eyes widened as I made to do exactly that. She reached across the table. "Jesus, not really. Sit down. What are you doing? Who cares whose ringtone it was? It's not like it's important."

"But what if it is?"

So maybe I overreacted and perhaps the alcohol exacerbated things, but *that* song after *that* video left me uneasy and what followed did little to calm my anxiety.

My dreams were strange that night. Though strange downplays it—see, it was a bastardised remix of that damn video and that damn girl. It was as if the video had unzipped my skin, slunk inside my tapered flesh, and become one with me. I appreciate I might sound like I'm off my fucking rocker but that's how it was.

The dream began near identically to the actual video but there was something off-kilter, something I couldn't place. It was the same and yet it was different—as if I was seeing the video through another lens, a filter where colours obscured and sounds scratched, slowed down, and amplified. As if they were grating up against my brain: neurological discombobulation. The fabric of the girl's fishnets scritch-scratched—sharp razors on a blackboard, raw friction as her legs crossed and uncrossed.

Crossed and uncrossed.

Crossed.

And.

Uncrossed.

Unsure if the video was slowing down or my brain shutting down.

I soon realised the legs had detached from the girl, but they weren't bloody or anything—hadn't been severed—they were perfectly smooth and polished: rounded out at the stumps.

Like they were meant to be.

Like they were better that way.

Scritch-scratch, scritch-scratch, louder and louder and fucking louder, until my ears wept.

I stuck a finger in my right ear canal, it squelched inside; sucked in by sludge—wet and slick. I removed my finger.

Examined it.

Smelt it.

Tasted it.

I didn't choose to do any of those things. They just were.

I had no control.

Control was an illusion.

Is, was, and always has been.

Next were the white lines, obscuring my vision, like the ones you see on badly recorded VHS tapes. Only this wasn't a recording, this was my actual fucking vision—my own eyes playing tricks on me.

The girl's legs reunited with her body and she danced.

Though it wasn't as I'd remembered. Wasn't as alluring, as sensual, as downright sexy.

Her movements awkward and rigid. As if the actions of her body were not those of her mind.

Her legs disappeared and she fell to the floor.

A cockroach on her back, arms frantically flailing.

And then—like it was nothing, like it was all just an act—her legs re-emerged and she flipped back up: a gymnast.

The white lines faded, my vision returned—brighter and better, saturation whacked way up—the girl began painting her lips, except this time *I* was the pot that housed her lacquer. My ear secretion, the varnish. Each time she dipped the brush in, it stung like vinegar on an open wound.

Tears streamed down my face.

She leapt forward.

Lips bigger than the room.

Opened her mouth and swallowed me whole.

SUNDAY JANUARY 24, 2016

By the time morning came the dream had receded to the back of my mind. I wandered downstairs, using the wall as a makeshift bannister to steady myself, trying to ignore the pounding in my head. Not in my twenties anymore—I was getting too old for this shit.

When I entered the living room, Rachel passed me a cup of coffee. "You look like crap."

"Good morning to you, too. Want to go out for breakfast?"

"I'd love to, but I'm running late—and surely you are, too. Isn't your start time eleven-thirty?"

I necked back some coffee, hoping it'd wake up my brain. "Start time? It's Sunday."

"Uh huh," she said, putting the finishing touches to her packed lunch: a chicken and walnut salad with homemade mayonnaise. "Two words: speaking clinic."

Bollocks, I'd forgotten all about it. Looked to my watch—double bollocks—I had to leave the house in half an hour. I gulped down most of the coffee. "Why didn't you wake me? Must have slept through the alarm."

"Well, you're thirty-one so should probably wake yourself . . . I did try, but you were out like a light."

"I feel terrible."

"I'm not surprised. If it's any consolation I don't feel so hot either, can't have had much more than a few hours' sleep."

"We didn't get back *that* late. We were in bed by midnight." I finished the coffee, knocked back a multivitamin with a tall glass of water.

Rachel stopped making her lunch and fixed her eyes on me.

"What? What did I do?" I said, looking at her properly for the first time that morning, noticing the grey shadows beneath her eyes.

"You don't remember, do you?"

"Erm, you're gonna have to help me out with that one."

"You woke me up with all that screaming—"

"Screaming? Get out of here!"

"I'm serious, I'd never heard you like that before. Hysterical doesn't do it justice. Fact is, you probably woke the whole neighbourhood."

"You can't be serious."

"I switched on the light to see what all the fuss was about—ready to give you a right what for—then I saw the blood gushing out of your ear."

"Oh, come *on*. Like that's gonna happen in my sleep. Stop pulling my leg."

"You were *wide awake*. Don't believe me? Check your right ear. Tell me, how is it today?"

"Hurts like hell. But so does my left ear, my head, my back, my whole body."

"You see? I tried calling an ambulance but didn't get very far."

"It's only three numbers. You flake out at two?" I grinned, she didn't.

"I got through but they were asking so many questions and my Japanese isn't great at the best of times, so I just screamed 'kyuukyuusha' and hung up."

"Why would you do that?"

"Because I panicked. I was freaking the hell out and you were getting worse—I wanted to help you, not to spend time on the phone. I wasn't thinking straight. Plus, I thought they'd be able to trace the call to our address but . . . " Rachel looked down. "Well, they didn't. I was so frightened. I had to shower and change you. You were near catatonic."

It sounded like an elaborate wind-up and yet Rachel looked serious, her hands shaking. I didn't fully buy into what she was saying, it made little sense not remembering any of that. Fact was, I hadn't even drunk that much. But it seemed an odd thing to make up. And besides there was no sense in lying about such things, no logic to it.

"Check the washing basket, Freddie."

I did, and sure enough, there lay my once pristine white t-shirt, the one with the V-neck, all smeared in blood. I held it up to the ceiling, like the stains were a trick of the light, like if only I got the right angle I'd see it wasn't bloodied at all.

"I don't understand. I really don't remember. God damn it, this isn't good. Isn't good at all. What am I supposed to do? Should I see a doctor? Is that the answer? Fuck . . . "

"Maybe. See how you feel. But if anything like this happens again, then yes, *absolutely* you should see a doctor."

I never did remember the bleeding or the screaming or the way Rachel had showered me down, but piece-by-piece, as I rode the Seibu-Shinjuku line to work, I remembered the previous night's dream, though it was a little hazy and merged with my recollection of the original video. My brain was getting scrambled, and I started to doubt myself, questioning what I'd seen in the video and what I'd seen in my mind's eye. I got out my phone, located the original video, and pressed play.

I felt voyeuristic watching it in public, and whilst the train wasn't busy and nobody paid me any attention, I still made a point of shielding the screen.

No blood. No dismembered legs. No girl on the floor shaking.

A weird video, for sure, and without a doubt it had an unsettling air, but it wasn't on the same level as the dream. I tucked the phone back into my pocket and rode the rest of the journey in silence, eyeing the other passengers—wondering if they'd seen what I was watching. Perhaps caught a glimpse in the window's reflection.

An elementary school kid with a yellow hat and Nintendo Switch kept peering up at me.

He knows, he definitely knows.

After some speaking clinic level-checks and a brunch of tuna onigiri, a banana, and black

coffee, I felt more human. Thanks to a last-minute cancellation, I had a two-hour gap in my schedule and intended on filling it with episodes of *Death Note.* I'd already downloaded a batch from Netflix so wouldn't have to use my fast-dwindling data. Getting comfortable, I poured another coffee, ripped open a bag of macadamia nuts, and loaded up the episode.

Then I got the Twitter notification: a new direct message.

A little odd given I'd disabled all social media notifications. Then again with near daily updates and frequent changes to terms of service I accepted with blind clicks, I might have accidentally turned them back on. Whatever the case, the message was brought to my attention and curiosity coupled with a weak will got the better of me.

Like the Instagram message from a few months previous, this was from a random. The display picture an identical Hello Kitty image. Adrenaline surged through my body. I turned the heater off, the room suddenly roasting, took a large gulp of water, and clicked through.

The text read: *Does this excite you?*

Followed by a Bitly link.

Given the anxiety the last message had given me I definitely didn't want to click the link and yet how could I do anything but? I pushed my phone and headphones into my pocket. I'd take a look, but not in the classroom where someone might interrupt me. What if it was another video and worse than the last? What if Akane or one of the part-time secretaries burst in asking me to complete long-neglected admin? Or worse, another teacher wanting help with lesson planning? Matthew was always asking for stuff—had a big heart but no confidence. Worse still, if a student strolled in unannounced. Just because nothing was scheduled didn't mean someone wouldn't crash through the doors—especially the younger kids. The kind of kids whose parents should probably keep them on a lead—not out of cruelty or as a punishment, just as a way of knowing their whereabouts. A GPS chip would do it, too, but a lead's more practical—cheaper, too.

I left the classroom, gave Akane a nod of acknowledgement, and headed towards the communal toilets the school shared with a travel agency. I locked myself inside a cubicle and clicked the link. Another video. My heart beat faster as it buffered.

A girl sat on a leather office chair, wearing a Hello Kitty mask identical to the one in the original video. Her lips were blood red, long jet-black hair draped to her left. She wore a plain black hoody, short black skirt, fishnets, high heels. Surely the same girl.

THE GIRL IN THE VIDEO

Same girl, same chair, same room.

This time the camera afforded a better view of the room. Posters on the wall, mostly musicians: Ulver, Scroobius Pip, Nine Inch Nails, Mastodon, Electric Wizard. An eclectic mix, yet all artists I liked.

The girl stretched out on the chair, rocking back and forth with an open-mouthed smile.

Posters aside, the room was minimalist and tidy. A western-style bed to the left, a simple wardrobe to the right. Presumably a desk in front of her. From the position and angle I reckoned the video was recorded via a laptop webcam.

The girl stood and leaned closer to the camera. "Wait." Her voice as soft as a kiss on the neck.

She walked off camera. Returned with an acoustic guitar. She perched forward—still smiling—and strummed fast simple chords.

Her face hardened and she broke into song, high-pitched punk screams:

"What do you like? What do you like?

"Tell me what you like? Tell me what you like?

"What do you like, do you like, do you *really* like— tell me what you like, what you like, what you *fucking* like.

"I wanna know, I wanna know, I wanna know, I wanna know, I wanna know, I wanna know, I wanna know, I wanna—"

I clicked my phone to check the video hadn't crashed, but it was still playing as it should, she just kept repeating the same line. Over-and-over. Each repetition more twisted than the last, punky shouts becoming black metal shrieks.

The girl picked something up from her desk,

around the size of a hole-punch, which perhaps it was. Then nonchalant, like it was no big-deal, she drove the object into her head. I heard it thunk against her skull. A single stream of scarlet trickled from forehead to lips.

She kicked her legs back with such force she crashed off her chair, the camera tracking her, though how I wasn't sure. My guess was it had a motion sensor or there was someone else, behind the camera. But what kind of a fucking loon would watch and record all of this?

The girl continued to sing and play the guitar, her screams indiscernible, piercing highs in time with erratic strumming.

A jerky cut and the video looped back to the start of the song and played over.

Identical.

Almost.

Until the end.

When she fell off the chair the second time, the camera failed to track her.

In quick succession:

A scream.

A deep voice, incomprehensible—*a man's voice?*

And a gunshot.

I nearly fell off the fucking toilet seat. The sound levels were way off and it shit me up worse than a barking dog in a bad horror movie.

After the gunshot, the video flashed forward to the girl, Hello Kitty mask covered in blood. She lay motionless on the floor, the camera lingered. Next to her sat a bloodstained machete. Which made no fucking sense given the gunshot, but did any of it?

THE GIRL IN THE VIDEO

The screen faded to black and the girl whispered: "Reply and tell me what you like. It's important." The video ended.

What the hell was I supposed to do with that? And who in the world was sending me these videos? And why? What was the point?

I had a whole lot of questions and a whole lack of answers. So I did what I always did when I had questions without answers and turned to Professor Google. I had an inkling this was some viral video series, so put in all manner of search terms to see if I could uncover others who had viewed the video. Words and combinations revolving around 'Hello Kitty', 'video', 'viral', 'anonymous', 'blood', 'gun', 'girl', 'fishnets', 'sexy', 'creepy', and so forth. With a Google search history like that I was definitely going on some sort of watch list, but this felt more important.

What I found were a lot of messed-up videos, numerous discussions on threads and forums about messed-up videos, but nothing on *my* messed-up video.

I played the video again, taking a couple of screenshots. Her face was always obscured by that stupid Hello Kitty mask but maybe—just maybe—this could give me a lead. I uploaded the clearest image to TinEye Reverse Image Search. It took 0.7 seconds to search 36.1 billion images.

No matches.

Shit. Now, what?

I considered uploading the video to YouTube, seemed like a good way to find out if anyone else had received the same video, and either way it might make me a little ad revenue—Christ knows the extra money would be useful, what with us trying for a baby.

But ultimately I decided against it. If the video had been deliberately sent to me, it seemed a violation to share it with others, to make it part of the public domain. True, I hadn't asked for the video, hadn't invited it into my life, but then you don't ask for gifts, do you?

A gift.

Was that what it was? A joke seemed likelier. Some dickhead from uni or my schooldays. Yes, a joke was most probable.

And yet there was something about that final line: "Reply and tell me what you like. It's important."

WEDNESDAY JANUARY 27, 2016

I'd wanted to hurl my phone out of the fucking window when the alarm blared out at 6 a.m., but seeing as I'd made a promise to myself the night before to up my exercise game and get a workout in before nine o'clock, I turned off the alarm, kissed Rachel on the forehead, and got out of bed.

I prepared a strong coffee in the French press and sat on an old deckchair in the almost-but-not-quite-patio outside, rubbing my cold hands together and looking up at the clear blue sky. I may have been exercising early, but I wasn't a total masochist—I'd ease into the day: caffeine and reading, *then* exercise. My sportswear was laid out on the exercise bench, my workout routine printed, and my playlist curated on Spotify. Matter of fact, I'd been so well organised I figured if I left it at that I'd already done 80% of the work and wasn't that what minimum effective dose was all about?

The morning started well enough. Up in my home office, with the portable heater on full blast, I dipped into David Lynch's *Catching The Big Fish: Meditation, Consciousness, and Creativity*. Don't get me wrong, I wasn't much of a creative person but I *was* a failing meditator. And besides, I had this hunch that if I read enough books on creativity I might one day *become* a creative. Now I'll hold my hands up and admit that ten years in it hadn't worked, but I was also an optimist and enjoyed reading about the creative process. That way I got to experience the high points vicariously without enduring many of the lows.

As soon as I turned the Wi-Fi on, the messages started flooding in, and the morning went to shit. Pro tip: if you want a chilled morning don't turn the fucking Wi-Fi on.

First it was Instagram, a comment on my most recent photograph, a well-lit shot of the burger I'd had at Shake Tree: "Tell me what you like."

Then it was a direct message via Twitter: "Tell me what you like."

Next it was a Facebook inbox message, which surprised me the most as I'd *thought* my privacy settings were maxed out, but whatever. "Tell me what you like."

Line: "Tell me what you like."

WhatsApp: "Tell me what you like."

Skype: "Tell me what you like."

Pinterest: "Tell me what you like."

Each message identical, each profile with that same Hello Kitty picture.

MICHAEL DAVID WILSON

Now sometimes when I turn the Wi-Fi on I'll open a shitty message, get involved in an online spat, or read a depressing newspaper article that affects my focus and stalls the morning's progress and with it my sense of calm. Though given I sometimes get angry at the alarm clock, or some prick queue jumping in the supermarket, I use 'sense of calm' pretty lightly. But all those simultaneous messages more than stalled progress. They were a full-on fucking assault and I was unable to focus on anything else.

Perhaps I'd clicked a link that had given away all my passwords and login details, infected my computer and smartphone with the 'tell me what you like' virus. It seemed like the logical explanation. Or at least as logical as I could muster so god damn early in the morning.

But a quick Google search returned nothing of interest.

I was still quick to change all my passwords and even set up a password management app—something I'd been meaning to do for months. Nothing like a near miss with a computer virus to kick some sense into me.

I scanned my various social accounts, making a point of checking outgoing messages, comments, statuses, etc. to ensure nothing untoward had been written on my behalf. Everything seemed in order. The only weird messages present had been sent consciously and of my own volition. Satisfied, I tweeted the following:

"Anyone know anything about this 'tell me what you like' spam that's doing the rounds?"

I hoped that would be enough for someone to shed

light on what was happening. Feign more knowledge than you have and often people will confirm your suspicions and then some. Works great with bullshitters, too. Catching them out at their own game.

I drank more coffee, listened to the latest Clutch album, and waited for the replies to flood in.

By the time Clutch had finished I'd received no replies and only one like. The 'like' was from a well-muscled blonde girl by the name of Amber-Marie. She had five followers, followed over 5,000 accounts, and according to her bio she was "look for big fuck NOW" and only posted periodically. Tweets like, "Someone push me on a big dIck please. #ClimateChange" and "I'm a virgin, and you? #JeremyCorbyn". I decided not to follow-up with Amber-Marie. I might have been working on my optimism but I wasn't *that* optimistic. And I didn't click any of her cloaked URLs either. See? I was learning.

It was gone nine a.m. when I started my workout. After a brief warm-up of stretches and bodyweight exercises, I picked up the cast iron kettlebell and started swinging. But I soon stopped—my heart wasn't in it. My body had already woken up and was unhappy with such a vigorous routine early-doors. I vowed to try again the following day. To wake up earlier and catch my body off-guard. Trick my way to a stronger, fitter, better body.

I finished work early and Rachel earlier still. When I returned home, I smelt the sweet aroma of the evening's dinner before putting my key in the door.

Inside, Rachel was setting the table. Courgette spaghetti and ground beef meatballs in a rich tomato sauce with various herbs, onions, and a smattering of cashew nuts simmered in the pan.

I undid my tie, rolled it up, and placed it on the coffee table. "Bloody hell, Rach, what a feast. How long did this take you?"

"Not so long," she said, serving the food onto large white plates.

"If you'd have called ahead I'd have got us a nice bottle of wine to go with it. In fact, if you give me five minutes, I can nip out and grab one."

"I wanted to surprise you. And besides . . . " she took a bottle of red from the fridge, a Chianti Classico, "we're already covered. And don't worry, it's not been in there long, just slightly chilled."

"You know, you really are an angel. What's the occasion?"

Rachel set the plates of food on the table. "Does there need to be one?"

"I guess not."

I opened the wine, poured generous helpings in tall chianti glasses.

As we ate we shared stories from our day at work and listened to jazz saxophonist, Kamasi Washington. The evening was going wonderfully and the wine had given me the most pleasant of buzzes, that blissful stage between sober and pissed—a warm hug for the brain.

"What was that status all about then? *Tell me what you like.*"

Ugh, if ugly was a phrase *that* was it. Felt nauseous just hearing it.

"It's probably nothing." I drank some wine, stuffed a big piece of meatball into my mouth, like if I filled it with enough food and drink I couldn't possibly continue talking. As if the subject might disappear.

"Hmm . . . probably nothing means *perhaps* something."

There was no getting past her, huh? Though I wasn't sure I should burden her with the videos and strange messages, I didn't want to make it into a *thing*.

"You can tell me. And if it's nothing then, hey, no big deal . . . but if it *is* something then I should know."

I scratched my neck, needed to shave my beard line back in. Looked Rachel in the eyes, no point in lying. Might as well come out with it. "So, someone sent me these videos. One the other day, one a few months back . . . they're pretty strange . . . You know, rather than explaining, it's best you see for yourself."

She nodded. "Well, no time like the present, pop them on."

"And spoil this great meal? No way."

"They scary?"

"Not exactly. Though the second goes a little bit *Too Many Cooks* towards the end."

"Ooh! See, now I'm interested."

I waved a hand dismissively. "Please, don't get your hopes up. It's not *that* kind of video—it's not especially entertaining and the production is . . . Well, let's just say, it's probably some dumbass kid fucking around."

Once Rachel had seen the videos, she sat in silence, phone still in hand, staring at its blank screen.

"Suffice to say, they won't be winning any Oscars," I said, trying to make light of the situation, whilst I finished the drying up.

Rachel sighed. "These are very odd indeed. Though I'm not sure I *get* it."

"I'm not sure there's anything *to* get."

"How did you say you got these videos again?"

"They were sent to me. Direct messages on social media."

"From?"

"That's what I'm trying to figure out. And honestly, your guess is as good as mine. Some anonymous account with a Hello Kitty display picture."

"Hmm, like the masks in the videos." She handed my phone back to me. "You think it's a joke?"

"Could be. Could be anything."

"One of your mates from uni, perhaps?"

"We were pretty dark, but this is a bit much. Besides, our idea of a joke was changing the desktop background to an extreme image or video. Goatse, lemon party, tubgirl, swap.avi—"

"All right, all right. Stop listing the websites already, you're making me picture them, you bastard."

"Blue waffle . . . "

She arched an eyebrow, her smile gone.

"Seriously, though, we haven't played jokes on each other for years."

THE GIRL IN THE VIDEO

"Which would make it the ultimate joke, you'd never suspect it."

"You find it funny then?"

"Not really. And not extreme enough for the total gross-out either, unless we're to believe the girl is *actually* dead, which obviously she isn't. It's so blatantly faked. But think about it, this was sent to *all* your personal accounts, even those with high privacy settings. Whoever sent them knows you. Have you shown the videos to anyone else?"

I shook my head. "Uh-uh. Apart from that Twitter thread, I haven't even mentioned it, and that came back blank, so . . . "

I huffed out a deep breath, exasperated. Hadn't mentioned the messages I'd received via Line and WhatsApp. As far as I understood it, you needed someone's mobile number to send a WhatsApp message and hardly anyone knew mine—hadn't got around to updating most of my mates since returning to Japan. As for Line, whilst privacy was questionable, I doubted my uni friends had even heard of it. I certainly hadn't before arriving in Tokyo. Still, I wasn't gonna burden Rachel with all that, didn't want to unnecessarily worry her. Not then. I'd do a little more digging and worry her if and when there was something worth worrying about.

The evening wound down. We drank more wine and watched *Mulholland Drive*. Every time the girl or video popped into my head I'd concentrate on my breathing, repeating mantras like "this too shall pass"

and "everything is temporary". Honestly, it didn't help. I still wasn't zen enough, whatever the fuck that meant. But I was trying.

After grabbing a shower, I headed upstairs, stark naked save for the blue towel I'd wrapped around my shoulders like a cape. When Rachel joined me, she wasn't impressed.

"Jesus, Freddie! The curtains are open, people can see straight through."

"Doubt it," I said, making my way to the adjacent room which looked out at the residents' car park.

"It was a statement, *not* a question."

"Who's going to be impressed by this, anyway?" I pressed myself up against the window, doing a little jig and rubbing my hair-clad chest against it before closing the curtains. I'd like to say it was because of the alcohol, but that would be dishonest . . .

"You're such a goof." Rachel closed the curtains. "A goof that's gonna get us deported if people catch you doing that kind of shit. And I don't know *why* you insist on wearing the towel like that."

"Just giving my fans what they like."

"Ha! Fans!" She smiled, turned the heater off, and slipped into bed. "Well, save a little energy for your biggest fan, huh?"

"Now *that*, I can do."

TUESDAY FEBRUARY 2, 2016

I was making a crab mayonnaise salad when I received the WhatsApp message: another unknown number, another Hello Kitty display picture. Every bloody time I'd almost forgotten about this oddball, another message would show up vying for my attention. I took a stand. Not this time—I was hungry, the message could wait.

After eating lunch and watching an episode of *Death Note*, my curiosity got the better of me and I loaded the message.

Always a Hello Kitty display picture, always a cloaked Bitly link, yet always a different account. What was that about? A way to hide their identity and locations perhaps? But, come on, let's get real—there are ways of concealing your identity online—it's not like a burner phone that you dispose of after a single use. Perhaps it was all part of the weird mind games. The appeal of it all, for her or him or them. Well, whatever, there was no point overanalysing. I opened the message: text that read, 'just for you'. I clicked the link and the video buffered.

A black screen with white text that read, "I know what you like."

Electronic music kicked in, something familiar— more upbeat and mainstream than Ulver. I'd listened to it whilst marking papers. Then I recalled— Deadmau5, *W:/2016ALBUM/*. Not the catchiest of album titles but damn good background music.

The black screen faded out, the inside of a train faded in. A number of passengers sat on green fabric chairs with grey plastic backs. They faced away from the camera. I couldn't be certain, but I reckoned it was England, possibly a London Midland train, like countless trains I'd taken before.

The next shot confirmed my suspicion: a cloudy

overcast day outside the Bull Ring in Birmingham. The camera zoomed in on the eyes of the iconic bronze bull statue. Lingered, then cut away.

The scene switched from day to night. Rain beat down outside Scruffy Murphy's, a rock and heavy metal pub I'd visited often as a student. Rockers gathered outside—smoking cigarettes and drinking beers under the shelter—shielded from the rain. In the far-left corner, next to a display of posters and promos, a gangly goth with lank black hair and a long leather trench-coat made out with a pink-haired punk who was so much shorter than him she had to stand on tip-toes.

Another cut. The lens fixed towards a bright blue sky. Clear, cloudless, and definitely not Birmingham. The camera jerked down awkwardly and focused on a statue, much as it had before. But this was different. A man on a horse—not simply a man, but a king. Underneath the king lay fallen snakes. Conquered.

The camera zoomed out to reveal the full scene—a bustling square in a European city. Another place I knew intimately: the Praça do Comércio in Lisbon. Rachel and I had spent many evenings nearby, drinking red wine until the sun went down as we looked out onto the Rio Tejo.

Lisbon faded.

A new scene in a dark room: the silhouette of a girl—*the* girl?—rocking in a chair, high-pitched feminine laughter.

Almost as quickly as the girl appeared, she flashed away, replaced by Yamato Station in Kanagawa, Japan. Not a video but a still shot, taken from the train platform and looking towards the ticket barriers.

THE GIRL IN THE VIDEO

A second still photograph focussed on a set of stairs that led to the first floor of an old building. A place I used to work. It had been a couple of years and I wasn't there for long, but it was definitely the school I'd taught at in Yamato. Though *school* was generous for a rented room in a block of other rented rooms. A remote place, away from the town proper.

Back to the previous scene: the girl in the rocking chair. "I know what you like, I know what you liiiike." She held the last syllable, taunting me, voice filled with glee, child-like. "I know what you liiiike."

A flash of white and red that lasted less than a second, too quick to comprehend.

Laughter as she see-sawed back-and-forth in the rocking chair.

The image died.

The laughter reverberating longer than the video.

"What *The Fuck* was that?" I said to the empty living room.

Technically it had been the most normal of the three videos I'd received. Banal even. And yet I was most unsettled. Each location, each place, was somewhere I'd been and was intimately familiar with. And not just places I'd been recently but over the years. Was that the point? Was that what the sender was trying to say? That this wasn't generic, wasn't viral. This was 'just for me'. He, she, or they knew where I'd been and *perhaps* even where I was . . .

I knocked back an L-theanine capsule with a glass of water to calm my nerves. I was getting ahead of myself, letting my imagination run wild with neither evidence nor substance. There was no proof anyone knew where I was. Furthermore, all the places in the video had been recorded on social media. Public posts on Twitter and Instagram, other people's public posts on Facebook. Anyone could have accessed them. I really would have to tighten up my security. Or, at the rate things were going, delete the bloody lot and be done with them.

I paused, sick at the realisation.

Anyone could have accessed them wasn't necessarily true. Yamato station, the school I'd worked at . . . I hadn't taken any photos or videos there, so . . .

My mouth was dry, heart thudding. I poured a large glass of water and glugged it down in one motion, held the glass tight, knuckles white.

Think.

Breathe.

Stay calm.

So, there *was* a possible explanation. Perhaps I'd inadvertently given away my connection to the school. All I'd have had to do was send out a public message with location services enabled. With the right know-how and determination, someone bothered enough could no doubt pinpoint my exact whereabouts.

They'd have to scour through posts going back years to find it. Who in the hell would go to such trouble?

The kind of person who'd make and send weird-ass videos . . . but who?

Someone I'd worked with during my first stint in Japan, perhaps? Truth was, I wasn't close to many people from back then—I'd worked hard, kept my head low, and spent most of my downtime exploring the country with Rachel. Added to which—how would they know about my university hangouts, my time in Portugal, the train I often took in England? It didn't make any sense.

The doorbell rang. Panicked, I lost my grip on the pint glass, sending the bloody thing to the floor where it shattered.

What if it was her? What if the girl in the video had found me? She'd tracked me halfway across the world, so why not to my current address?

I crept towards the heater remote, turned it off, its whirring stopped. The room as quiet as possible. I stood silently in the living room making like I wasn't in. Hoping that whoever was at the door would fuck off ASAP.

I didn't have many friends locally and fewer still who knew where I lived and being as Rachel was at work and had presumably taken her key, it couldn't have been her.

So, the girl in the video had shown up to punish me for not replying. She'd asked what I liked and I'd ignored her repeated requests. It was time to pay.

A second ring of the doorbell.

I looked to the back door. I could easily get out that way—through the crop fields and onto the river path. But what if that made things worse? Ignoring messages was one thing but legging it was quite another. Perhaps if I spoke with her we could work something out.

I heard movement behind the front door, some kind of rustling.

Then a loud assertive knock.

A man's voice called from beyond, something about a parcel.

So not the girl then.

I let out a long sigh of relief. Answered the door, trying to steady trembling hands—adrenaline still coursing through me—as I signed for and took the package from the delivery driver. The driver looked concerned but was too polite to say anything.

I closed the door, examined the package—Rachel's Amazon order—then collapsed at the bottom of the stairs, heart thudding against my chest. Couldn't help but grin. Then laugh. Soft chuckles at first, then a little louder, a little manically, a little high-pitched. A little like the girl in the video.

Once my heart rate had normalised and hysterics abated, I returned to the video, pausing on the penultimate frame. That flash of red and white I'd been unable to decipher the first time round.

It wasn't what I'd expected.

Now, honestly, I'm not sure what I *had* expected but whatever expectations I'd had weren't met: a close-up of modestly-sized milk white breasts, 'find me' written from left-to-right in blood-red makeup.

I closed the video quickly, like I'd been caught with my hands down my pants.

My phone lit up, a new text message. "I have more photos if you like . . . ;)."

What the shit?

This time there was no Hello Kitty display picture and no attempt to disguise the number either. Just a regular Japanese mobile number.

What impeccable timing, though . . . What on

earth were the chances? Unless she had a way to track each time I watched the video? Shit, was that possible? *Oh double shit!* The message had been an iMessage which meant she'd got a read receipt.

More photos, though . . . I felt myself stiffen. What the hell was wrong with me? The girl was scaring the crap out of me and yet my dick still stirred. I needed to get it together and fast. I turned the Wi-Fi and data off of my phone to make sure I didn't send any more read receipts and got ready for work.

That night I dreamt about the girl in the video again, but this time it wasn't creepy. It was a good dream, a pleasant dream—a fantasy, even. At least in the beginning . . .

In the dream, I lay in bed, staring up at the ceiling, searching for patterns amongst randomness. I reached towards Rachel but she wasn't there. All I found were cold sheets—Rachel's side of the duvet pushed back. The bedroom door opened and the girl from the video entered sporting her usual Hello Kitty mask. I craned my neck, drinking in all her details: low-cut black top, black skirt, suspenders, high heels. The girl threw the duvet all the way off, climbed onto the bed, and crawled towards me on all fours. She took my hand and gently pressed it to her warm wet sex. I hardened.

The girl threw her head back and laughed. "I told you, I know what you like."

She mounted me, pushed me inside her, and sang. "Tell me what you like, what you like, what you like . . . "

She felt divine.

The perfect fit.

My muscles relaxed and I closed my eyes, concentrated on her smooth slickness.

Her celestial sensation.

With each thrust she went a little faster, deeper, warmer—pushing me towards the divine.

But then her singing mutated. Became more frantic, until it was panicked, until she was flat-out screaming.

I opened my eyes.

Blood poured from the eye slits in her mask.

The bed floated on a river of blood as we headed towards the ceiling.

"Save me," she whispered

A solitary gun shot.

Her head exploded.

I shot bolt upright in bed, body soaked in sweat.

Rachel stirred, rubbed rheum out of her eyes.

She reached out towards me, felt how wet my chest was. "Whoa, you're burning up, you have a fever or something?"

"I'm okay."

She sat up next to me, accidentally brushing against and feeling how hard I was. "Oh, wow, you *are* okay." She gripped my cock. "Want me to take care of that for you?"

A slow solitary nod of the head.

But as she took care of things, all I could think of, all I could hear, was the girl singing.

THE GIRL IN THE VIDEO

SATURDAY FEBRUARY 6, 2016

It was happy hour at The Hub in Shibuya. I nursed a Jim Beam highball. The place stank of cigarettes, bad perfume, and desperation. I'd headed there straight after work, mostly because I needed to get out of the house and socialise more, to ensure the few friends I had in Japan remained friends. Honestly, though, it was easier to stay in and be complacent, I had enough mates back in England. Though as Rachel would often remind me: "This isn't England, Freddie. We need *connections* here." I didn't know what we needed 'connections' for but I supposed some friends would be nice. But as someone who was trying to moderate his alcohol consumption it wasn't easy. No one wanted to go for a glass of water or walk around the local park. It was all about boozing. Least it was with the teachers I'd met. Which was why I'd asked my colleague, Marty, if he wanted to grab a drink that evening. Now admittedly, Marty was a bit of a dick with loose morals and a simple borderline sexist, racist, misogynist, every other fucking-ist way of viewing the world. Rachel had met him once and couldn't stand the guy, but hey he liked heavy metal and was often free, so there was that. Given how much he hated other people I was surprised he'd ever left his hometown, let alone moved to another country, but here he was and there I was, next to him, because he was a *connection*.

"You ever had girls you haven't met send you strange videos?"

Marty almost spat out his beer. "You what, mate? That's a hell of a jump from Fetus."

That was true. We'd been talking about the death metal band, Dying Fetus, and how they were due another album soon. But then the alcohol had kicked in. Less filter—more think it and say it.

"That came out wrong. I'm not talking about sexting or any shit like that, not talking about spam either. What I'm asking is if you've ever had any girls—girls you've never met—send you personalised videos?"

Marty sparked up a Marlboro. "Like a sex thing?"

"No, *not* like a sex thing. What did I just say?"

"But a sexy video?"

"Umm . . . I mean, not traditionally sexy."

"Hey! No judgement here, brother. If it's sexy to you, that's cool. You do your thing. I've jacked off to some fucked-up shit before. Really nasty unpleasant business. After I'm done, I look at the browser and feel fucking disgusted with myself. I'd give you specifics, but if this place is wired . . . well, you know what I'm saying, I don't want to go to prison."

I cocked an eyebrow, unsure if he was making a bad joke.

"But let me tell you this, brother. If girls you don't know are sending you sexy videos, that sounds like spam."

"Personalised videos, Marty. Videos only for me."

Marty exhaled rings of smoke, tapped ash into the tray. "That's what they *want* you to think. But this isn't the noughties, they've got good at spam. They'll find all sorts of information about you, make it look legit, but you're just a number. One in hundreds of thousands. Know how?"

He'd got the wrong idea, but there was no stopping him.

"Data mining." He held up his smartphone, tapped it like he was the first one to come up with this shit. "This device right here is tracking everything. Your computer, too. Unless you're disabling location services, viewing websites through a VPN, taping up your webcam, disabling your microphone, making sure your calls and messages are secure etc. etc. then you're vulnerable and even then . . . Put it like this, brother, if people want to know about you, they'll *know* about you. In this room, there's a 99% chance of government cameras and microphones. I'm talking CIA, FBI, NBC, all listening in."

"In Japan?"

"You'd be surprised."

"Wait . . . isn't NBC an American television network?"

Marty grinned, open-mouthed, leaned across the table, voice low. "That's what they want you to believe."

"You're a fucking head case, Marty."

"A thin line between genius and insanity, was Mother Theresa who said that. Or was it Henry Rollins?" Marty put out his cigarette. "Point is, whoever said it, they *knew* what they were talking about."

"Fairly sure neither one of them said *that*. Anyway, we're getting off track—"

"So steer us on course, pilot. You've got this." Marty clapped his hands high in the air, so drunk he almost missed. Marty clicked his fingers twice in the direction of the bar. "Hey! Waiter! *Sumimasen!*"

"What the fuck are you doing?"

"When in Tokyo, mate. When in Tokyo . . . " Marty winked.

A well-dressed barman with short cropped hair and a goatee came to the table.

"*Nama futatsu kudasai.*"

He noted down Marty's order and went away again.

"I hate that shit. Calling waiters over with your fingers like they're your fucking slaves, it's draconian. Just walk to the bar, it's five seconds away . . . "

"Like I said, brother, when in Tokyo. And besides, I got you a beer so don't worry about it."

"I don't even drink beer."

"Well, now, you do. Kanpai, motherfucker." He chinked his old beer glass against mine. "Anyway, what's all this about girls and videos?"

I shook my head. "You know what, forget it, mate. You were right, it's a sex thing."

It was well past happy hour and I was feeling worse for wear. No way was I confiding in Marty—the more he drank the more bollocks spewed out his mouth, and the more I disliked him. No good would come out of telling him about the girl in the video.

Marty was in the toilet when the text came through.

"I know you liked the videos. Why so shy?"

The same number I'd received a text message from earlier that week, but this time, with booze inside me, I showed less restraint. Replied straight away. "Why don't you fuck off?"

THE GIRL IN THE VIDEO

I put the phone back on the table: face down, sound off. I wasn't gonna deal with her bullshit. At least not then. My body temperature was rising, I tried to steady my trembling knuckles.

When Marty returned he could tell something was up.

"You look like you've seen a ghost, mate." He pulled his phone from his pocket, slapping it down on the table.

I gazed at it, what if . . . ? Nah, surely not—whoever was sending the messages knew things about me from way back. Marty and I weren't even connected on social media, and I didn't reckon he was smart enough to pull that kind of shit. And yet I had received the text message mere minutes after he'd left.

"Nice phone," I said, staring right at Marty.

"Was one of the cheapest handsets Softbank had and still cost me an arm and a leg, fucking rip-off merchants."

"Bet it's good at sending *text messages* and *videos*."

"Um, yeah, obviously, given that this isn't the noughties I'd say so. It does the job."

"Sent any videos lately?"

Marty blushed. An admission of guilt?

I put my hand out. "Show me."

"What? Fuck off, I'm not showing you my videos, there's private stuff in there."

"Private stuff involving girls perhaps?"

The red in his cheeks deepened.

"Or *a* girl, should I say. A girl in a Hello Kitty mask, perhaps?"

Marty frowned. "What the fuck are you going on about? Why would there be a girl in a Hello Kitty mask? There's some sex stuff on here, sure, but nothing like that. Is that your thing then? Do you have a Hello Kitty fetish or something?" He pushed the phone towards me. "There's some good stuff. Guess you can look if you really want to."

I relaxed. It was dumb to have even considered Marty might have been involved. Paranoia playing tricks on me, blurring reality. I handed him his phone.

"What is it, mate? Are you gonna cry?"

I wasn't gonna cry, at least I didn't think I was, but it was nice to see Marty had a tender side. Truth be told, it was the first time I'd seen him express anything vaguely resembling empathy. I wound up explaining everything, or at least trying to—the alcohol and anger muddling things.

"Sounds like she's a proper psycho, brother. One of your exes no doubt."

"I've been with Rach for getting on a decade. Last girlfriend I had I was only just out of my teens."

Marty shrugged. "Then some bird you're fucking. I'm telling you, some of these Japanese chicks have a screw loose, this one time—"

"I'm not fucking anybody else."

The folds on Marty's forehead furrowed like he didn't understand. He stuffed a handful of crisps into his mouth. "Well, suit yourself. But you're missing out, brother. Not fucking a Japanese chick while you're in Japan . . . I mean what next? You gonna tell me you haven't tried sushi? Haven't gone to karaoke?"

"Piss off, Marty."

"I'm just saying . . . Besides, it's not healthy to go most of your life with one partner. Your testosterone might be high now, but it won't always be that way—take advantage, brother."

"I said. *Piss. Off.*"

"All right, all right. Don't get your knickers in a twist."

"You haven't listened to a word I've said. You know what, Marty. Fuck this place and fuck you, too." I necked back the beer, threw down a couple of thousand yen notes, and left the pub.

As I walked to the station, passing revellers in fancy dress—because every day's a party for someone in good old Shibuya—I wondered if I'd been overly dramatic, perhaps even a little harsh to Marty. He was a simple guy, an ignorant guy, an annoying guy who said some dumb shit, but he wasn't a wholly bad guy. Problem was he wasn't a very good guy, either. Well, whatever—what was done was done. I didn't give enough of a shit to go back and apologise. I'd clear the air with him the following week, or, if he kept sinking beers back he'd likely drink so much he wouldn't even remember.

I reached for my phone to check train times and find out whether I was walking or running for my Takadanobaba connection. My phone illuminated: over twenty missed calls all from the same number. I didn't need to check who they were from, the influx of text messages confirming my suspicions.

MICHAEL DAVID WILSON

1) Don't talk to me like that.

2) I know who you are and I know where you are. I always have.

3) Say something Freddie.

4) Don't ignore me!

5) You're making a big mistake. Pick up your phone.

6) I have something I want to show you, I think you'll like it.

7) Thank you for the other night, I saw what you did for me.

8) You and me, we could be something special. This is the start of something incredible Freddie.

9) I can give you what she can't.

10) Be careful Freddie! Don't fuck with me! I can be dangerous. You don't know who you're dealing with.

11) Sorry. I just want to talk to you. I have something to show you.

12) Nothing? What the FUCK? Watch this video. Then call.

She'd attached the aforementioned video to the message. I started the download as I approached Shibuya crossing—a mixture of commuters with briefcases and revellers with cameras and smiles, paraded across the road like circus clowns. Far too fucking happy. I nearly punched an American tourist in a Van Halen t-shirt, the prick was waving his hands up in the air, shouting about how 'amazing' life was, and getting in my way.

By the time the Yamanote line train arrived the video had downloaded. I couldn't watch it right away as the train was rammed. When people talk about

THE GIRL IN THE VIDEO

Tokyo trains being packed like sardines, that's not hyperbole, that's how it is and how it was. In front of me stood a young woman in stilettos, smelling of floral perfume, her head practically resting on my shoulder. Behind me, a businessman whose perfume was 100% cigarettes and whiskey. To either side stood school children, kitted out in full uniform, despite the time, complete with rucksacks and sports bags almost as tall as they were.

Hordes of passengers poured out of the train at Shinjuku and I quickly secured a seat. Admittedly I snatched it away from a Junior High School kid who was nearer, but she simply hadn't honed the art of seat acquisition on busy trains. She looked dejected afterwards, sought solace in her Nintendo Switch. *Well, whatever, kid, you've got years ahead of you, you'll perfect it eventually, that or get used to rejection. Either or—life's tough.*

I loaded the video.

Rain beat down outside Atsugi station. The sky a white sheet. The camerawork shaky and handheld. Video quality not especially good—probably shot on an old phone.

The camera made its way up the road and away from the train station, passing the Indian restaurant and independent coffee shop I'd often visited not long after arriving in Japan.

Stopped at the intersection: straight for the Sports Park, right for Hon-Atsugi, left for Ebina.

Made a left.

Past the old bakery.

Past the turn-off for Create Superdrug Store.

Past the multitude of vending machines that peppered the street like road markers.

At the martial arts school and independent supermarket, the camera turned right and headed towards an apartment block.

My old apartment block.

I'd lived in a cramped 1K there when I'd first arrived in Japan.

The camera shot up towards the second floor—*my* floor—lingered, then cut out.

A new scene. Evening. Black skies and heavy rainfall. The focus: a house with the lights on, both upstairs and downstairs. There was no mistaking it, the *second* place I'd lived in Japan.

"You're in there," a soft off-camera voice said. The audio somewhat tinny, but it was a voice I knew, that had sung to me in dreams and videos. Her voice hardened. "But so is she."

The camera cut off abruptly, replaced by a sharper image of higher quality. An evening walk alongside the Karabori river, street lamps and house lights illuminating the path. A girl—*the* girl—hummed a tune off-camera. Passing the elementary school on the right, the junior high school on the left. She rounded the corner and made her way into the residents' car park. The camera tracked the houses, left-to-right, then right-to-left.

Settled on a house.

102.

My house.

"This is live, Freddie," the girl said.

THE GIRL IN THE VIDEO

She walked around to the back of the block. Stopped at my door. Inside the living room light was on. The camera panned the washing, hanging on the line outside. She reached a hand out, touched a pair of black boxers. "Yours," she said, then tutted. "They're getting wet, Freddie."

From behind the back door I heard music: Lady Gaga. And if I listened carefully, if I really strained, I could hear Rachel singing along.

"She's in! She's in!" The girl's voice an ecstatic squeal.

The camera jolted, faced the floor temporarily, the view switched.

The camera no longer directed towards the back door, it now faced the camerawoman.

The girl in the Hello Kitty mask.

She held up a thick blade, some kind of machete.

"You need to take me seriously, Freddie. I have something on you, something you thought you'd buried a long time ago. So don't fuck with me and don't go to the police . . . unless you want your wife to spend some time with me and my friend." She waved the blade, then broke into laughter. "Bye-bye!"

As the video finished, the train pulled into Takadanobaba. I raced to the Seibu line, making my connection in under a minute.

Standing room only. I leant against the door connecting one carriage to the next.

Heart pounding, head full of noise.

Takadanobaba was still half an hour away from Kumegawa and from there it was a fifteen-minute walk to the house. I had to do something *now*. Kept ringing Rachel but she wasn't picking up.

51

Because she's dead. Because that psycho bitch whose messages you've ignored has got to her.

No, that wasn't true. Couldn't be true. There was no way.

She'd said, in so many words, Rachel would wind up dead *if* I went to the police, *if* I fucked with her. I'd done neither. So Rachel wasn't dead.

Yeah, because psychopaths are known for their moral codes and playing by the rules. This isn't fucking Dexter, *mate. Ring the police!*

But if I rang the police and she killed Rachel . . . how could I live with that?

And yet if I did nothing and she killed her, anyway . . . how could I live with *that*?

I was fucked.

There was no right choice, only a sliding scale of wrong ones.

"Are you okay?" A twenty-something woman with a kind face tapped my shoulder.

I tried to reply but no words came out, just incomprehensible grunts, tears streaming down my face.

She passed me a tissue and I dried my eyes. Blood stained the white tissue red.

"Your nose." She handed me more tissues.

I cleaned up the nosebleed. The woman backed away, receding into the crowded train.

I tried ringing Rachel again. Sweaty fingers barely hitting the right keys.

This time she picked up.

I slid down the door to the floor, whole body shaking.

"Hey you . . . hello? He-llooo? Freddie? Freddie? Is something the matter? Freddie? Hello?"

THE GIRL IN THE VIDEO

"Rachel."

"Yes?"

I snapped to attention, adrenaline kicking in. "Lock the doors. Lock the fucking doors right now."

"Huh? What are you talking about? I'm making tagliatelle."

"Lock the fucking doors, Rachel!"

"The doors *are* locked. They're always locked. Why wouldn't they be locked?"

"Check them!"

"Okay, okay . . . " I heard her move from the living area with the whir of the heater and background music to the quieter hallway. "Yes, the doors are locked."

More footsteps, music again, back in the living room.

"You need to stay in the house . . . or perhaps you need to get out of the house. Fuck . . . I don't know. Thing is, there's a psychopath on the loose, but I need you to stay calm."

"What are you talking about? A 'psychopath on the loose'? Is this one of your jokes? Or a strange euphemism? What's going on?"

An old man with a walking stick hobbled over, tried to get my attention. "Please, no talking on the train."

"Fuck off."

"Huh?"

"Not you, Rachel. Stay calm. Let me figure this out."

"I'm calm, but I don't understand. You're not making sense."

"The girl in the video, she's real, and she's outside the house. She has a knife, she wants to hurt you."

53

"What?"

"The video, the girl—she's fucking mental, Rach."

"I can't understand you—the signal's breaking up and you're speaking too fast. You mean the girl in the Hello Kitty mask?"

"Oh Christ, you see her?"

"Erm, no. But I remember the videos. Very strange indeed."

"How can you sound so calm?"

"You *literally* just told me to stay calm. Not that I really understand. Listen, I don't think there's anyone here. Let me have a look." I heard a door creak open, footsteps down the corridor.

"No! What are you doing?"

"Checking the peephole. There's no one there. Just cars."

"Round the back—she's round the back!"

"Let's see . . . "

"No! Do not open the fucking door. She'll cut you. I swear to fucking God, you cannot open that door."

"Okay, okay, I'm not opening the door. But if what you're saying is true, I should call the police."

"No, you can't do that."

Someone pulled at my shirt sleeve. I looked up, it was that bloody man with the walking stick again. "Mister, could you please . . . "

"Fuck. Off."

"Who are you talking to?"

"Sorry. Some old cunt keeps telling me to get off the phone. Are you sure you're safe? Are you sure she isn't there?"

"As far as I can tell."

"Look, I better go. Don't want to get kicked off the

fucking train. But make sure all the doors and windows are locked. Better yet, barricade them. Arm yourself with a weapon—a knife or something. And *don't* call the police. I'll be there as soon as possible."

I hung up.

Forehead sweltering, vision blurring.

Lightheaded, like I might pass out any minute. I looked to the old man, standing next to me. Scowling. A bottle of mineral water peeked out of his coat pocket. I grabbed it, necked the lot. "Thanks, mate."

The old codger didn't look pleased.

I felt the weight of the other passengers' scorn for the rest of the journey. Saw the occasional glimpse up from a mobile phone or tablet, only for them to return their attention back to their screen with overly dramatic gestures.

I sent Rachel numerous text messages to check she was hanging in there. She quickly replied to each. If she sensed danger she didn't show it—didn't ask why I'd asked her not to call the police, either—was pretty blasé about it all.

Once my heart rate had calmed and vision settled, I wrote a text to the girl. "What do you want?"

She replied almost instantly. "You."

I stared at the screen. The fuck was I supposed to do with that?

Another message flashed through. "Tomorrow 3 p.m. Harajuku. Next to GAP. Go there. Call me. No police or else."

When I arrived home and saw Rachel—alive and beautiful and radiant—I held her so close and so tight she had to push me off of her. "You're hurting me."

"I love you so fucking much."

After checking the house and surrounding areas outside and coming up empty, I headed back inside where I collapsed on the sofa. I explained everything to Rachel—showed her all the videos, the text messages, even the calls from the girl in the video.

"We're ringing the police right now," Rachel said.

"We can't. Don't you see? She's blackmailing me."

"Blackmailing you with *what*?"

"That's just it, I don't know—it could be anything. Says she has something on me, something from a long time ago."

"That's *ridiculous*."

"Is it, though? Christ knows how, but she knows where we live and places we used to live, too. Is it such a stretch that she knows something from the past that could fuck me over?"

"She's not got anything on you because there's nothing to *get on you*. Right?"

My face flushed. I'd done a lot of stupid shit in the past.

"Right?" Desperation in her voice, a touch of vulnerability, too.

"Just don't call the police. Let's play along for now. I'll go to Harajuku tomorrow—see if anything comes of it. Then, depending on what happens, I may or may not go to the police *after*."

Rachel shook her head. "I don't like the sound of this. Not one bit. What if it's a trap?"

"Harajuku's busy, what's she gonna do in a crowded place in broad daylight?"

"Who knows? But I don't like that she *could* do something. She knows who you are and what you look like—you know next to nothing about her. And what you *do* know—what *we* know—is terrifying. She turned up here, at our apartment, with a fucking machete!" Rachel paced the living room, clutching a glass of red wine. "What if this isn't about getting you to Harajuku but about getting *you* away from the house and me?"

"I'd never thought about it like that."

"You're not thinking at all."

"But, wait, if she wanted to strike when I was away she could have done so tonight. She chose not to . . ."

Rachel put the glass of wine down on the table, folded her arms. "Either way, I don't feel safe here. We should sleep somewhere else tonight."

"Where?"

"Someplace she doesn't know about. Christ, what if she is *they*? What if there are numerous people behind the video?"

"I think it's just her."

"Based on what?"

I looked to the ground.

"Based on fucking *what*?"

She pushed me hard in the chest, then fell into me, sobbing and shaking as I held her tight.

"I'm so sorry. For all of this, I'm so very sorry." I tried to keep my voice steady, to stay in control, to remain strong. "I think we should stay put. She isn't in the house, we know that at least. We're safe here. Safe inside the house." I kissed the top of Rachel's head and stroked her hair, her tears and whimpers abating.

If we left and the girl was somehow keeping tabs on the house, she'd see us leave and might well follow us. And without a car, we'd be out in the open for a good while—exposed and vulnerable. Yes, on balance, staying inside the house was best.

Rachel got up from the sofa and poured her wine down the sink. She took a packet of coffee from the cupboard.

"What are you doing?"

"I'm clearly not getting any sleep tonight." Rachel heaped a spoon of coffee into the French press.

"Don't be silly, this is my mess. I'll stay up tonight—you shouldn't have to suffer . . . any more, that is."

"Unless there's something you're not telling me, this isn't your fault either. Besides, I won't be able to sleep with this . . . this . . . this *knowledge* of a fucking psychopath roaming around." Rachel poured water into the kettle, set it to boil. "I really would feel better if we spoke to the police, though, or at least spoke to *someone*. Isn't it safer that way? Suppose she attacks both of us, suppose she *worse* than attacks us, who would know?"

Rachel made a decent point, but who to tell? There was always Marty, who was halfway to knowing anyway, but he was a drunken fucking idiot and might not remember come the morning.

"I'll call Hillary," Rachel said. "And forward her all the videos, too."

"What if she calls the police?"

"How's she going to call the Japanese police from the UK?"

"I don't know, but I imagine it's possible . . . I don't think you should call her."

"Because?"

"Because she freaks out about everything, blows little things completely out of proportion. And this right here is no little thing. This is a fairly fucking big thing. Trust me, she will freak out." I stood up, helped Rachel finish making the coffee. "The situation we're in, it's fragile. Scrap that, it's *volatile*. One wrong move and who knows what will happen."

"I'm calling Hillary."

"Can you trust her?"

"She's my fucking sister, of course I can trust her."

Rachel tried calling Hillary several times, via Skype, but for whatever reason she didn't answer which I was thankful for. I crossed my fingers Rachel would forget about Hillary. At least until after Harajuku.

Rachel kept bringing up the police, but honestly, I wasn't sure what good it would do. Hadn't dealt with the police in Japan but had heard less than glowing stories about them.

And okay, I hadn't dealt much with the police in England either. Just the once when some twat had lamped me in a pizza shop because he didn't like the way I looked at him. He was a known criminal, but no one had been prepared to testify and the police told me he'd said I'd hit him, too, so with no witnesses it was his word against mine, never mind the bruise on my eye or permanent astigmatism.

I hadn't bothered with the police since.

Rachel and I spent the rest of the night downstairs, awake for much of it, old episodes of *The*

Inbetweeners and *Peep Show* playing in the background. It might seem messed-up to put a comedy on at a time like that, but we couldn't stand the silence and it was a welcome distraction from reality.

Fatigued and exhausted, we flittered in and out of sleep. Periodically I'd jolt upright, afraid someone or something stood in the room with us. Through squinting eyes I'd scan the room, but I never saw a thing.

SUNDAY FEBRUARY 7, 2016

At 6:30 a.m. I conceded I wasn't getting any more sleep and got up. Rachel was already in the shower, though there was no singing amongst the pitter-patter of water.

By the time Rachel emerged, I'd made us a big vat of coffee and had ground beans ready for a second. It was that kind of morning. Rachel wore a grey hoodie and black leggings, there were bags underneath her tired eyes, and she'd made no attempt to conceal her exhaustion with makeup. Which was how Rachel often rolled, her outward appearance projecting her inner feelings. It was an honest way to live. We sat on the sofa, sipping coffee, Tangerine Dream playing in the background—we weren't really listening but it gave us something other than our inner thoughts and turmoil to focus on.

Rachel took my hand. "I've got something I need to tell you. I've been going back-and-forth on whether to say anything, but it seems right— it might change what you do and don't do today."

I adjusted my slouch to a more upright position. "I'm listening."

She took something from the front pouch of her hoody, placed it on the coffee table in front of us. My eyes followed. A pregnancy test, a thin blue line on the display which intersected with another to form a cross.

"It's only faint, but it's definitely there. I took a test yesterday, and another this morning, to be sure. I'm pregnant."

I rubbed my eyes. I was drained and exhausted, veering towards broken thanks to the girl in the video. I looked to Rachel, then to the test. It was real all right, not another messed-up dream—it was actually happening. "And you're sure about this? You're sure you're pregnant?"

"Yes. The strength of the line depends on the hCG in your urine and the sensitivity of the pregnancy test. But it's there. It's *positive.*"

"Not one of those phantom pregnancies then?"

"Well . . . I suppose it *is* possible. We'll book a hospital appointment this week to confirm the pregnancy, but I have a really good feeling about this. I'm pregnant, Freddie. *We're* pregnant."

I pulled Rachel closer and held her tight, held her like it was forever.

With fatherhood looming, complying with the girl in the video seemed more important than ever. On the way to the train station, I listened to dark drum 'n' bass and pored over what I'd say and do if I ever came face-to-face with the girl. As I approached the entrance, someone slapped my shoulder from behind. I spun around, fists raised, which wasn't how I'd ordinarily greet someone but what can I say? It was no ordinary day.

I lowered my hands when I saw him. "Marty?"

He was sweating profusely and smelt of waste, as if someone had dunked him head-first into a toilet, which I supposed was possible, he had a habit of getting on the wrong side of people.

"My man!" he said, stale alcohol permeating the air.

His eyes were bloodshot, his hair sticking up at all sorts of angles.

"Jesus Christ, you started on the booze early."

"Never really stopped." He grinned.

"Well, good for you, but I need to get going."

He jogged after me. "Hold up, I have something. Been waiting all morning to give it to you."

"How'd you know I'd even be here?"

He shrugged. "Lucky guess, hombre."

"Hombre? Dude, shut the fuck up and get out of my way."

He pushed something into my hand, a USB stick.

"I've been thinking about what you said about that video and I reckon this might help."

Adrenaline kicked in. Heart thumping quicker than the drum 'n' bass I'd been listening to. "You know something about the girl in the video?"

"Yeah," he slurred. "Brother Marty's got you covered."

THE GIRL IN THE VIDEO

I heard a train pulling into the station but stayed staring at Marty. I lowered my register. "So, what is it? What did you find?"

I cursed myself for not having my laptop with me. I often carried it in my rucksack in case I got some free time, but I'd figured with everything going on, that was the last thing I was gonna get today.

"This is what you like."

What I *like*.

Tell me what you like . . .

"Marty, are you *involved* in this?"

"I'm your wingman, bro."

"What the fuck are you going on about? That doesn't even make sense. Listen, I need you to tell me everything. How are you involved? What do you know? What's on this stick?" I waved the USB in front of his face and he followed its rhythm. "I *need* to know."

Marty belched. "This is just a man helping another man out. You need your fix and I'm your dealer, baby. We're talking girls in Hello Kitty masks, girls in masquerade masks, some dressed up as anime characters, even got some furries, and let me tell you that shit gets a lot more hardcore than you'd think. There's even something involving a horse—I mean, I'm not sure if that's your deal, I threw that one in for fun."

"I don't—"

"It's all on the stick—almost two gigs' worth. Aren't you gonna thank me? Buy me a beer or something? That right there's top quality kitty clunge."

When it dawned that the stupid bastard had just

compiled a load of animal- and anime-themed pornography, I could have floored him then and there. But instead I simply shook my head, gave him a quick "fuck off, Marty" and ran to platform one.

I got into Harajuku early and spent much of the morning and some of the afternoon in Jonathan's family restaurant where I got wired on coffee and tried eating some food. But alas, I had no appetite and too much worry—about why the girl in the video was doing this, about what she had on me, about Rachel, about her phoning Hillary, about the pregnancy, about raising a child—whether I was capable, whether I was worthy of fatherhood, whether it was reckless to bring up a kid in a world with so much violence, corruption, abuse, and cruelty.

At a loss as to what else to do, I tried meditating.

Like, *really* tried.

But it was no good.

I was restless and agitated and couldn't sustain watching my breath for longer than thirty seconds at a time.

Instead, I wound up re-watching all of the videos the girl had sent me, taking notes in the hope I might uncover some clue, some hidden meaning that would help me make sense of it all.

That if I watched close enough, looked hard enough, everything would become clear.

But it didn't.

I uncovered nothing.

At around noon, Rachel rang suggesting we go to the police together. She sounded shaky and panicked, said that with a baby on the way things had changed and we couldn't afford to play by the rules of some strange girl. We needed to do things the proper way.

I understood her reasoning and agreed with her— one wrong move could prove fatal.

But I'd made my decision and was sticking with it.

I stayed put.

Rachel's call left me more on edge. She hadn't said it explicitly, but I'd known she was pissed off with me. At best she thought I was naïve, acting like this headcase girl was someone I could just talk things out with. At worst Rachel thought I was selfish—putting myself ahead of her, our marriage, our unborn child. But that wasn't how I read the situation. In turning up at our house, armed with a bloody machete, the girl had proven she was unhinged, that she wasn't the sort of person to play chicken with—call her bluff and she might do something terrible, she might harm Rachel for no greater reason than she could.

I topped up my coffee, hands shaking, sloshing the liquid over the top of the mug as I settled back at the table. Was there any conceivable way this could still be a prank? I'd seen the girl, the blade, my apartment, and even heard Rachel, too. But with computers and technology you could near enough fake anything. I didn't think it was a joke and yet I found myself dialling Henry, the biggest technology whizz I knew, one of my best uni mates, and responsible for some of the most insane jokes back in the day. If anyone knew how this shit could be pulled off, it was Henry. I hadn't spoken with him in almost a year—probably it was the coffee, the adrenaline, the sheer fucking absurdity of it all, but I felt I needed to.

The call took a while to connect and longer, too, for him to answer, but eventually he did.

"Hello?"

"Duuuuuude," I said, a mixture of real and feigned enthusiasm.

"Who is this?"

"Freddie . . . "

Momentary silence then movement from his end, footsteps. "Dude, it's almost four in the morning, what do you want?"

"Ah, shit, I'd forgotten about the time difference. Should I call back?"

"Is this important?"

"I think it could be . . . "

"Go on then, you get me up this early you should at least come out with it . . . "

I stalled. Henry wasn't as mellow or jovial as I'd expected, which given I'd woken him up at no-fucking-way-o'clock was understandable.

"What's going on?"

"I don't know, man, but I was hoping you could help me out. I'm scared, mate."

A kettle whistled on Henry's end.

"Freddie? You still there?"

"Yeah. Sorry. Shit. I don't even know where to start."

"Well start somewhere. You didn't wake me up for nothing, did you?"

"You remember how at uni we'd change each other's backgrounds to Lemon Party and shit like that?"

"Uh-huh." Henry poured water.

"And sometimes we'd create mash-ups, weird videos, like the time you spliced Geoff's birthday party video with Meat Spin and Swap.avi?"

He chuckled. "Classic—took a long time. But come on, lad, cut to the chase."

"You don't happen to know anything about the girl in the video, do you, mate?"

"In Swap.avi? Weren't there four of them?"

"Not in Swap, and yes there were four . . . I think I'm being targeted, dude. Someone's sending me these weird videos, blackmailing me, showing up at my house and—"

"Have you been drinking?"

"Freddie, it's only just gone one in the afternoon."

"So, is that a yes or no? Back in uni we'd—"

"I haven't been drinking, dude."

"And you're still in Japan, yes?"

"Right. These videos, they have things about me— where I've lived, what I've done, bands I like—that not a lot of people know. Don't think there's anyone who knows *all* these details. Doesn't make sense, dude."

"So, you think I did it because ten years ago I changed your desktop background to Tubgirl? That's what this is about?"

"No! Jesus, dude, why would I . . . I mean . . . I don't . . . but . . . Well, I mean, are you involved?"

"Fuck off, man. Of course, I'm not *involved*. You're off your head."

"Listen, I'm not doing a good job of explaining. Yesterday the girl came to the house with a machete. She was threatening Rachel."

"Holy shit, is Rachel okay? Dumb question, I know,

obviously she's not okay but . . . Hang on, you think *I* sent a girl in Japan round your house with a god damn machete to threaten your wife? What the hell is wrong with you? We've done some crazy things but not *that* kind of crazy. That's Ted Bundy levels of psycho right there."

"That's not what I'm saying. I don't think you did that. Of course you didn't do that, you would never do that, but—"

"But what?"

"Well, maybe you made it *look* like that. You faked a video or something, plus, um, a phone call . . . "

"You honestly believe that?"

"I'm done knowing what to believe. I'm getting strange personalised videos, I'm getting threats and—"

"Go to the police, dude."

I sighed. "I mean, that's what Rachel said, but . . . "

"Rachel's smart. You have someone threaten to take you out with a machete, you don't just wake up your mate in merry old England at four in the fucking morning, you call the police. It could be a matter of life or death"

"That's what I'm afraid of. I mean, the girl specifically said *not* to go to the police."

"Name a criminal that encourages people to go to the police."

"Now, let's see . . . "

"Don't *actually* name one. Listen, Freddie, I'm sorry you're going through this, but I don't know what you think I can do from here. How can I help?"

He was probably right. Likely I'd made things worse, looked like a right fucking loon. But then I remembered Hillary. "Rachel has a sister, Hillary, she lives up in Yorkshire. You remember her?"

"Um, no."

"Well, anyway, Rachel was thinking about ringing her and—I mean, fuck, dude, Hillary will just convince her to go to the police and I'm telling you, that just isn't a good idea in this situation."

"Okay, and?"

"Look, I know this is a longshot, but maybe if I gave you Hillary's address you could watch her or something?"

"Watch her?"

"Or tap her phone, that way if Rachel calls her I'll—"

"Dude, stop talking. I don't even know where to begin with this. How about the fact I live in Reading and Yorkshire is what? Over two hundred miles away? Four hours in the car—"

"I could help with the petrol money if—"

Henry's laughter cut me off. "Stop. Talking."

"I know it sounds crazy . . . "

"Yes, Freddie, it *does* sound crazy. I'm gonna go now. Mostly because I don't want you to keep making things worse, but you have to talk to Rachel. Communicate with her. You've been married a long time—I'm sure you don't want to resort to tapping her phone. I thought you two had a good relationship."

"We do, but—"

"Then keep it that way. And honestly, mate, you should go to the police. Keep me posted."

Henry hung up.

I replayed the conversation several times wondering if there was anything I could have said or done for things to have gone worse. The phone call was supposed to be productive. A way to figure out how the videos had got to me, what the girl wanted, how I could avoid things escalating. A conversation to reassure me and make me feel better about myself and the situation. I'd failed on every level.

I ordered the biggest, most expensive dessert and scoffed it as quickly as I could.

I left Jonathan's with plenty of time to get to the meeting spot. As always, Harajuku was rammed. Tourists and locals jockeyed for position as they made their way up and down the busy streets.

At five to three I stood outside GAP, phone clutched tight, waiting for the girl to make her next move. My eyes darted between my phone, the station entrance, and either side of the street.

No sign of her.

Honestly, what did I think would happen? That she'd race around the corner in broad daylight wearing her trademark mask?

I didn't know what to think anymore.

And, quite frankly, I was fed up of thinking.

Was beyond thinking.

Was too tired to think.

Perhaps if I'd been thinking it wouldn't have come to this. I'd have gone to the police after she'd first contacted me. But instead I thought nothing of it and even got off on watching the video. Made me feel sick just thinking about it, but it was the truth.

Should have gone to the police . . .

But who goes to the police over a strange video? What crime had been committed? I imagined how it might play out: "What you showing us that for, mate? Enjoy it. Maybe next time she'll invite you over for a private session, know-what-I-mean?"

Speaking of the police, there were a lot of them about. I'd seen police around Harajuku before but never in such force. Clad in uniforms of different shades of blue: formal jacket and matching trousers, button down shirts, stab vests, duty belts, and white gloves. The women wore bowler hats, the men peaked caps. Two officers stood on the pavement across the road from me, next to Harajuku Station entrance.

The clock struck three.

No message, no call, no anything.

What was going on? I was where she'd asked me to be. What was the next step?

Another minute elapsed.

I started to write a message to the girl, to ask what now, to tell her I was ready and waiting, had followed her instructions to the letter. But I couldn't get the tone right. Kept erasing each attempt. Sometimes too needy, other times too acerbic, too desperate, too flaky.

Fuck it, I'd wait it out even if it killed me.

Some stocky man in a red t-shirt approached, holding a sales board listing various items of clothing and prices. "Hey, bro! Come with me, got some great deals, you'll love it."

"No thanks." I scrutinised my phone, as if engrossed in an important message, though I was clearly staring at the home screen.

"*Amazing* sales—fifty, sixty, even *seventy* percent off." His eyes widened as if such a discount had never occurred before.

"I'm busy."

"It's your style, bro. You can't miss it."

I looked to the board: Adidas, Nike, Reebok, and various other sportswear. It sure as shit wasn't my style.

"No thanks."

"Bro, you gotta get in on this." He grabbed my wrist, I flinched away, instinctively swung a right fist at the man, who narrowly bobbed out of the way.

"Fuck off!"

"A'ight, a'ight, easy bro." He raised his hands up in peace, like he was fucking Gandhi or something, and backed away. "Maybe another day, yeah?"

The would-be salesman retreated, blending into the crowd. I tried to concentrate on my breath, to lower my heart rate, to calm down.

Deep breaths. In . . . then . . . out. In . . . then . . . out.

Let the negative thoughts pass and the positive remain, negative thoughts pass and the positive remain, negative thoughts pass and—*seriously, who the fuck did that dickhead think he was? Touching me like that. Fucking wanker.* Let the negative thoughts pass and the—oh to hell with it.

My phone rang. Still full of anger I answered quickly. "About fucking time, you bitch."

"Freddie?"

"Oh, shit. Sorry, Rach, thought you were . . . Listen, darling, I really can't speak now, the girl could ring any minute now."

"You shouldn't answer like that."

"No, you're right. It's just this dickhead was . . . You know what, forget it, but I really should hang up."

THE GIRL IN THE VIDEO

I looked across the road at the police. "You might be right about going to the police, you know."

She exhaled. "Oh, Freddie, I'm so glad you think so. Truth be told I . . . "

"Truth be told you what?"

I looked down—bloody signal had gone. As soon as it returned my phone lit-up, an incoming FaceTime call from the girl in the video.

"Hello," my voice weak. I saw my face before I saw hers. Christ on a bike, I looked ten years older than this morning.

When the video finally connected the camera didn't face the girl but rather some nondescript street in a residential area. Her breathing heavy, the camera shook as she walked.

"You blew it," she said.

My stomach turned. "What? I did everything you asked. What are you talking about? I haven't fucking blown anything." It came out angrier than I'd expected, which was honest. I *was* angry—was royally pissed off with this girl and her infantile bullshit.

She didn't respond, continued walking, rounded the street corner, passing a series of vending machines. As she walked she swung a machete out in front of her. The camera had to be attached to a headset. The machete was thick and dull grey, likely the same one she'd brandished the previous night.

"Look, I did everything you asked, so put the machete down, and grow up!"

She laughed, not giving a fuck about my renewed confidence.

"Where are you going?"

But it was then that I recognised the back streets

and grey concrete buildings. She was in Yamato, heading towards the school I'd worked at a couple of years back. The school I'd glimpsed in one of her videos.

"I should call the police! Walking around near a fucking school with a machete—you head case."

She started humming 'Twinkle, Twinkle, Little Star' as she approached the school.

"Going around like that in broad daylight—Christ almighty, what's wrong with you?"

"Twinkle, twinkle, little star. How I wonder what you are."

"If anyone sees you, you're getting arrested."

"Up above the world so high, like a diamond in the sky."

"I did everything you asked," I repeated, trying to sound more reasonable.

"Maybe. But your bitch of a wife didn't!"

"Leave Rachel out of this, she's done nothing wrong."

She sighed. "I'd have been so much better for you, Freddie. And I really *really* wanted to kill her. Like, I actually dreamt about it. Many times. Maybe dream is the wrong word. Fantasy, perhaps, because I often woke up wet. Sometimes I'd stab her which was especially exciting—much more satisfying than a gun. With a blade, you really feel it, there's a weight to what you're doing, you know? It wasn't always like that. Sometimes I was more passive, poisoning her food and drink—classic stuff. But you want to know my favourite? Pushing her in front of a moving train. That was a real thrill."

"What do you want?"

"But no matter how much I think about it, the conclusion's always the same, I just can't kill her. Because you love her." She spat on the ground. "Ugh, so silly. *You* love *her*, even though she can't give you what you want, and *I can*. But, *whatever*, this is the next best thing."

She took the stairs up to the first floor of an old building, heading towards the rented room in which I'd taught a handful of classes.

"I don't understand. You're not making any sense."

"Soon you will." She held the machete up in front of the camera.

I prayed this wasn't what it looked like. That she wasn't *that* fucking stupid.

"There could be kids in there," I said, anger once again diminished, my voice a shrill husk.

"Yeah." Another laugh.

I fumbled with my phone, needed to record the call, in case she did something truly awful, evidence for the police. I'd heard of people recording FaceTime calls before but there were no obvious settings.

Fuck.

I had to stop her, to reason with her, to keep her talking—that's what they do in the films and television shows, they keep the would-be criminal talking so they don't do anything rash.

"Just hold on a minute. Just stop. Make me understand. Help me understand."

"That's what I'm doing." She held the machete so close to the camera I could see the light reflecting off of its thick sharp blade. "Patience please."

"Not like this, there has to be another way."

"Not anymore. We've exhausted all possibilities."

"This doesn't make any fucking sense!" So much for reason and calm. I was attracting quite the crowd as I screamed my voice hoarse, concerned passers-by glancing in my direction. If only they'd known, perhaps they wouldn't have been so apathetic.

There were still two police officers across the road, outside Harajuku Station. I pushed forward through the crowd, waited for a gap in the traffic to cross.

"I'm going to the police," I said. "*Right now*, I'm going to the police. You hear me?"

"She already did. That was your final mistake."

She? Rachel. Oh Christ . . .

"I told her not to," I said as if the girl would give a shit. "You have to believe me."

The girl slammed her fist against the classroom door.

"Don't open the door! Don't open the door! Don't open the door!"

"They can't hear you," the girl said, so cool and so calm.

I crossed the road, practically threw myself in front of the two policemen. "Look! Look! *Mite! Mite!*"

One of the cops placed his hand nearer to his right trouser pocket. *To his gun?* I forced my phone into the hand of the taller of the two policemen who looked at the screen.

We all did.

We all saw as the twenty-something fresh-faced man with the crop of blonde hair opened the door. Baby-faced and energetic, a beaming smile to greet all of his students. We saw, too, as that smile reversed. As warm enthusiasm turned to cold fear. Saw his eyes

THE GIRL IN THE VIDEO

widen and his face age years in seconds. Saw his song of innocence transformed into a scream of experience as the blade plunged into his stomach.

Then the call disconnected.

I don't want to think about what happened next. I relive it every day, the news footage burnt into my mind's eye, perpetually playing.

As soon as I revealed the girl's location, police were dispatched to the school. But they were too late.

There was no girl.

Just remnants of a massacre.

Pools of blood on the floor and spatter up the wall.

Reading about each death and seeing the photographs broke me then and breaks me all over again with each recollection, but I'll lay it out as best as I can. There were seven fatalities, one adult and six children, which was about as much information as the mainstream newspapers gave, but I uncovered the rest, including the names of the victims, via the Dark Web. Matthew McCain, aged twenty-four, lay motionless in the entranceway, his smartphone in his hand, '110' on the screen, dead before he'd hit 'call'. Next to the whiteboard lay Akito and Takeo Suzuki, aged seven and eight, little hand in little hand. Hanging over the window ledge, like she was trying to escape, was eight-year-old Momoka Oshima. On the ground below lay the youngest victim, Miyu

Suzuki, aged six, clutching a bloodied My Melody teddy bear. The final victim, Hiroki Yamada, aged eight. My heart sank. I'd known him, had a drawing of his on my fridge. He'd locked himself in the bathroom. The lock, a rusted single latch, had been busted off. Sitting on the toilet, in soiled clothes, his decapitated body. Neither reports nor videos of the crime scene revealed the location of his head.

The following was written on the whiteboard:

I want to go to Disneyland.

I want to eat ice cream.

I want to be happy.

If there was a God in this world, if there was justice, that's where they were and that's what they were doing.

But how anyone could reconcile a God with a scene like that I did not know.

The police took me to the station for further questioning as they tried to trace the assailant and uncover the identity of the girl in the video. I rang Rachel who was quick to join me. It turned out she'd arrived in Harajuku a little after one o'clock and had been using 'find my iPhone' to track my whereabouts all day—had been just streets away when she'd phoned.

"Please don't be mad, darling."

But I wasn't mad.

How could I be?

I was empty.

Numb.

THE GIRL IN THE VIDEO

Shell-shocked.

Broken.

But not mad.

She told me, too, that after finally getting through to Hillary, she'd visited our local police box that morning. Armed with copies of the videos and messages—copies she'd made while I was getting showered and dressed—she explained everything as best she could. Of course, the police hadn't taken her seriously. At that point what was there to even take? The death threats had been via the telephone call, of which there was no record. The videos and messages were disturbing and at times aggressive—*"Don't fuck with me! I can be dangerous. You don't know who you're dealing with"*—but nothing explicit. I didn't know if there was even really a crime. Something related to stalking or harassment, perhaps? Though how seriously either was taken here I wasn't sure. Still, to their credit, the police took notes. Notes which would later help identify the girl in the video. Though how the hell the girl knew Rachel had contacted the police remained a mystery.

As the days became weeks became months I learnt more about the girl in the video. Though why she'd done what she'd done, why she'd chosen to send me the videos, and why those specific videos, wasn't so clear. I could speculate and had speculated, but the answers were never wholly satisfying.

The girl in the video was Yuki Yamanaka. After that day, she was never again 'the girl in the video' or 'the Hello Kitty girl', both of which sounded far too cutesy. Nor was she simply Yuki, which suggested a closeness we didn't have, or a human side I doubted.

Yuki Yamanaka was a twenty-year-old university student living with her parents in Yamato, Kanagawa prefecture. It came out that for a brief number of months, some years back, I'd been her after-school English teacher, though the name was unfamiliar, and I couldn't recognise her from the photographs that appeared in the media, though I'd never forget her again. She had distinctive wide eyes with a depth that frightened me. She was the nail that stuck up and refused to be hammered down.

I might not have remembered her, but, as her internet history would reveal, she remembered me.

Though *remember* wasn't quite right.

I had never receded into her past, had always been a part of her present. She'd checked out my social media accounts several times per day for getting on four years. Had visited profiles of my friends and family with lesser privacy settings, presumably in the hopes of glimpsing a photograph, video, or insight into my life. It turned out that she'd visited both Portugal and England, though whether the videos in each location had been recorded personally was not confirmed.

Yuki Yamanaka was neither caught nor seen after the Yamato School Massacre, as it was soon known, and various theories spread which Rachel and I discussed but never wholly bought into. Some said Yuki Yamanaka's parents were in on it and were harbouring her someplace, others said she'd fled the country, and others still theorised she'd soon turned the machete on herself, unable to live with what she'd done to those kids. The latter stunk of big-time bullshit, how that would happen without a body made no damn sense—and a machete suicide? Come off it! This wasn't hara-kiri—Yuki Yamanaka had no honour. Still, I'd gone over the practicalities of that one numerous times with Rachel. Like, if Yuki Yamanaka was really gonna kill herself, how would she go about it? We settled on an overdose, hanging, or simply throwing herself off a tall building. Though if she wanted to go the scenic route there was always a god damn mountain. I'd started reading up on it and scanning the newspapers and web for unidentified suicide victims, just in case. You jump off something just three times your height and it's fatal fifty percent of the time.

Three times your height.

That's all it takes.

Yuki Yamanaka hadn't taken her life. Not as far as I knew.

Besides, I had an inkling that true monsters like Yuki Yamanaka were incapable of such remorse.

Amongst the horseshit and speculation, there were even whispers it had been a terrorist attack perpetrated by the Islamic State. Though for once ISIS didn't rush forward to claim responsibility and a thorough search of Yuki Yamanaka's home uncovered no evidence to support such a theory.

Some fucking imbeciles even said there had never been a massacre, that the entire thing had been staged alongside Matthew McCain, who was not only the teacher at the school that day but, so it went, Yuki Yamanaka's lover. It had been a ploy to allow the two to elope to a distant island and start a new community with the children. Not only was there nothing to suggest that Matthew McCain knew Yuki Yamanaka, let alone had been her lover, but the grieving parents and bloodied bodies painted a different story.

Rachel and I soon moved north of Tokyo, to Tochigi prefecture, where we attempted to start life afresh. Not taking any chances, we deleted all our social media accounts, sold our computers, phones, and anything else which could connect to the internet. We did our best to erase our digital footprint, though of course it was impossible. With time, I built us a basic computer, we only went online to Skype family members, via a VPN, and new nonsense-name account. We bought basic prepay phones for emergencies.

I developed a deep fear of technology and the connected world we live in and at times was close to walking out and going truly off-the-grid, afraid that even having a registered address, bank account, and health insurance was too much. But as strong as my fear was, I couldn't put Rachel through it.

I'd already done enough.

Too much.

So I saw a therapist, which helped lessen the nightmares and sleep paralysis, but knew I'd never fully recover because I was incapable of unseeing or un-experiencing what had gone before.

I considered leaving Japan, thought it would be for the best, but Rachel reminded me that living in Japan had been *our* dream and if we left, Yuki Yamanaka won.

But she had already won, or at least I had lost, and I was all out of dreams.

I stayed put for Rachel.

Kenichi was born in October of that year giving

me a sense of purpose and joy I hadn't experienced in months. Rachel and I both enjoyed glimpses of happiness that had been long absent, albeit more tired and fatigued than before. I'd quit teaching after the Yamato School Massacre and, with an infant son to look after, settled into the role of full-time house husband, citing Kenichi as the reason for my teaching hiatus, though we both knew my social anxiety and fear of leaving the house were the real drivers.

WEDNESDAY OCTOBER 18, 2017

I'd been getting better—leaving the house more, taking long walks in the park, attempting small talk with strangers in cafes. Occasionally I'd even reason that the Yamato School Massacre wasn't my fault, that I couldn't have foreseen or prevented it. But those thoughts were quickly replaced with other darker images—bloodstained teddy bears, headless children, unfulfilled dreams set in ink on the whiteboard. If I'd just played along, if I'd just told her what I wanted, and given her what she wanted, this could have been prevented. Or if I'd not opened the messages, if I'd not clicked the links, if I'd not . . .

But I had.

I had done all of those things and more.

Which brings me to today: Kenichi's first birthday.

Like I said, I'd been getting better, right up until half an hour ago, when I opened the door to discover a shoebox-sized package on the doorstep. There were no signs of the deliverer and at the time I didn't think much of it, scooping the package up and placing it in the living room next to the other presents, ready for the grand opening as soon as Rachel and Kenichi returned from the supermarket.

Then I saw the Hello Kitty sticker next to the address.

Lightheaded, I steadied myself against the television stand, and counted my breath—which I've finally gotten good at—to save from passing out.

I tried to convince myself that the Hello Kitty sticker was just a trigger, that the package was perfectly innocent. After all, it was addressed to Kenichi and Hello Kitty stickers were hardly difficult to come by.

And yet the only people who knew our address were close relatives and Rachel's employer.

Presents from family had arrived weeks ago.

I ripped open the package, shards of brown paper decorating the floor like confetti.

The box was empty, save for a single DVD inside a transparent case which sat on a bed of bubble wrap.

Scrawled across the disc in black pen: Bitly.

With trembling hands, I took the disc from its case and pushed it into the PlayStation. The video played automatically.

White text on a black screen: 'I want you to want me.'

The scene opened in a white-walled room.

Bare, save for a single chair in the centre.

A girl skipped into the room wearing a Hello Kitty mask—*the* Hello Kitty mask, now infamous. Positioned over her right shoulder was an acoustic guitar.

THE GIRL IN THE VIDEO

Yuki Yamanaka.

She sat on the chair, cleared her throat, and strummed the guitar.

"Happy birthday to you.

"Happy birthday to you."

I tried not to think about the faces of the children she'd slaughtered, to stop everything from coming back, to suppress the self-hatred, the shame, the guilt of it all.

But the thing about trying not to think about *something* is you always think about it.

"Happy birthday dear Kenichi."

I was close to hurling. Couldn't get six-year-old Miyu Suzuki out of my head, her My Melody teddy bear daubed in blood, held so tight and so close to her little lifeless body.

"Happy birthday to you."

After her performance, she threw her head back and cold unfeeling laughter filled the room.

Laughter I hadn't heard in a long time.

And laughter I had never stopped hearing.

She placed the guitar on the floor, stood up, strolled towards the camera, and leant forward so that the Hello Kitty mask took up the entire screen.

Her voice a whisper. Like it was our little secret. "I still have something on you, Freddie. Better play nice this time." She stood back, picked up the guitar, and squealed. "Bye for now."

Resumed her playing, her singing, her dancing. Skipped across the screen: a deranged Eminem.

"Guess who's back?

"Back again.

"Kitty's back.

"Tell a friend.

"Guess who's back, guess who's back, guess who's back, guess who's back, guess who's back, guess who's back . . . "

The video faded out.

Must have been the way the morning light from beyond the frosted patio sliders caught the box but there appeared to be something else glinting beneath the bubble wrap. I turned the box upside down. The bubble wrap tumbled out and I saw it fully.

Frayed at the edges and worn, the Hello Kitty mask.

Dark maroon specks peppered its white cheeks.

I thought I was gonna hurl, but managed to keep it down, to remain composed.

I stood up, surveyed the living room, noting everything Rachel and I had built together, stopping at the photograph in the olive frame next to the television. The three of us. Kenichi in my arms, Rachel by my side. All smiles in Arashiyama forest, surrounded by gorgeous towers of luscious bamboo, greens of every shade. My favourite place in the world with my favourite people in the world.

Everything I ever wanted.

The reason I returned to Japan.

My life's purpose.

But as long as Yuki Yamanaka was alive it wouldn't be enough.

We'd never be safe.

Never be happy.

Smiles only surface level.

I knew what I had to do.

Not just for me, but for us.

THE GIRL IN THE VIDEO

For Rachel.

For Kenichi.

I wrote a quick note to them—a note they would understand. Then walked up the two flights of stairs to my attic-office, the third and final floor of the house. Calm and clear-headed for the first time in a long time. I picked up the large bottle of Jack Daniels from atop the bookcase, took a large swig, and opened the sliding doors to the balcony.

I'm standing on the balcony now. Looking up at the blue sky, the crisp cool wind kissing my face, the fresh dew-scented air filling my lungs.

For once, I feel alive.

For once, I feel the moment.

I step closer to the edge, look down at the grey swathe of concrete below.

Take a long deep breath and let the energy of the earth swim within me.

Whatever I do, wherever I go, Yuki Yamanaka will always find me.

Whether awake or asleep she will be there.

And she will always have something over me.

The power of possibility. The power of what if.

Her words echo, her words always echo: *I still have something on you, Freddie.*

Say it and it becomes true.

Becomes reality.

She has everything and she has nothing. All the dark secrets untold.

All the guilt and the shame and the self-hatred

and the lies I've told others, even the lies I've told myself.

I cannot let her win.

I cannot be consumed by the darkness any longer.

I want to be set free.

To set my family free.

You jump off something just three times your height and it's fatal fifty percent of the time.

That's all it takes.

At six-foot tall the odds are in freedom's favour.

Another deep breath—the best yet.

This is my decision, my move, my salvation.

I cross myself and roll the dice.

"I'm sorry, Rachel."

ABOUT THE AUTHOR

Michael David Wilson is the founder of the popular UK horror website, podcast, and publisher, This Is Horror. A professional writer, editor, and podcaster, Michael's work has appeared in various publications including The NoSleep Podcast, *Dark Moon Digest,* LitReactor, *Hawk & Cleaver's The Other Stories*, and *Scream*. The book you are now holding, *The Girl in the Video*, is his debut novella. His second novella, *House of Bad Memories*, lands 2021 via Grindhouse Press. You can connect with Michael on Twitter @WilsonTheWriter. For more information visit www.michaeldavidwilson.co.uk

If you enjoyed *The Girl in the Video*, don't miss these other titles from Perpetual Motion Machine . . .

LOST SIGNALS
EDITED BY MAX BOOTH III & LORI MICHELLE

ISBN: 978-1-943720-08-8

$16.95

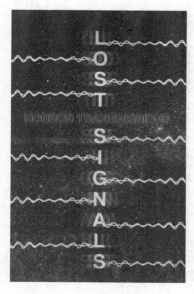

What's that sound? Do you feel it?

The signals are already inside you. You never even had a chance.

A tome of horror fiction featuring radio waves, numbers stations, rogue transmissions, and other unimaginable sounds you only wish were fiction. Forget about what's hiding in the shadows, and start worrying about what's hiding in the dead air.

LOST FILMS
EDITED BY MAX BOOTH III AND LORI MICHELLE

ISBN: 978-1-943720-29-3

$18.95

From the editors of Lost Signals comes the new volume in technological horror. Nineteen authors, both respected and new to the genre, team up to deliver a collection of terrifying, eclectic stories guaranteed to unsettle its readers. In Lost Films, a deranged group of lunatics hold an annual film festival, the lost series finale of The Simpsons corrupts a young boy's sanity, and a VCR threatens to destroy reality. All of that and much more, with fiction from Brian Evenson, Gemma Files, Kelby Losack, Bob Pastorella, Brian Asman, Leigh Harlen, Dustin Katz, Andrew Novak, Betty Rocksteady, John C. Foster, Ashlee Scheuerman, Eugenia Triantafyllou, Kev Harrison, Thomas Joyce, Jessica McHugh, Kristi DeMeester, Izzy Lee, Chad Stroup, and David James Keaton.

THE GREEN KANGAROOS
BY JESSICA MCHUGH
ISBN: 978-1-943720-42-2
$18.95

Perry Samson loves drugs. He'll take what he can get,
but raw atlys is his passion. Shot hard and fast into
his testicles, atlys helps him forget that he lives in an
abandoned Baltimore school, that his roommate
exchanges lumps of flesh for drugs at the Kum Den
Smokehouse, and that every day is a moldering
motley of whores, cuntcutters, and disease.
Unfortunately, atlys never helps Perry forget that,
even though his older brother died from an atlys
overdose, he will never stop being the tortured middle
child.

Set in 2099, THE GREEN KANGAROOS explores the
disgusting world of Perry's addiction to atlys and the
Samson family's addiction to his sobriety.

The Perpetual Motion Machine Catalog

Tales from the Holy Land | Rafael Alvarez | Story Collection
Tales from the Crust | Various Authors | Anthology
The Nightly Disease | Max Booth III | Novel
The Tears of Isis | James Dorr | Story Collection
The Train Derails in Boston | Jessica McHugh | Novel
The Writhing Skies | Betty Rocksteady | Novella
Time Eaters | Jay Wilburn | Novel

Patreon:
www.patreon.com/pmmpublishing

Website:
www.PerpetualPublishing.com

Facebook:
www.facebook.com/PerpetualPublishing

Twitter:
@PMMPublishing

Newsletter:
www.PMMPNews.com

Email Us:
Contact@PerpetualPublishing.com